TWO MEN IN A BASKET

TWO MEN
IN A
BASKET

AND OTHER STORIES

COLIN BARKER

Matador
Unit E2 Airfield Business Park,
Harrison Road, Market Harborough,
Leicestershire. LE16 7UL
Tel: 0116 279 2299
Email: books@troubador.co.uk
Web: www.troubador.co.uk/matador
Twitter: @matadorbooks

ISBN 978 1 80313 566 3

British Library Cataloguing in Publication Data.
A catalogue record for this book is available from the British Library.

Printed and bound by CPI Group (UK) Ltd, Croydon, CR0 4YY
Typeset in 11pt Aldine by Troubador Publishing Ltd, Leicester, UK

Matador is an imprint of Troubador Publishing Ltd

To Carel.

CONTENTS

TWO MEN IN A BASKET

'I hope you know what you're doing,' said Cynthia to her husband Trevor and his brother Errol looking at the huge balloon on their wrecked lawn. She pulled her cardigan tightly around her shoulders for it was still chilly that June morning only an hour since dawn with the sun not yet up. She yawned, for she'd already cooked them a full breakfast, kept the coffee coming and cut sandwiches for the flight, now tucked away in plastic containers and safely stowed in Trevor's backpack.

Watching the pair struggling to manoeuvre the huge wicker basket or 'gondola' nearer to the deflated balloon she thought how thankful she'd be when the whole business was over and having witnessed so many mishaps in the past she merely sighed when Errol, missing his footing, fell headfirst into the folds of the huge envelope.

'Why didn't it come inflated instead of just *lying* there?' she'd asked them during a coffee break.

'What's the fun in that?' Trevor had replied, but since then it didn't seem they'd been enjoying themselves one little bit.

Her anxiety about the project had begun the previous day when two lorries arrived outside the house with the balloon and its basket and what seemed like miles and miles of rigging and ropes. She'd gasped when she saw how *big* it was and had a sneaking feeling that her view was secretly shared by the boys.

They'd watched in silence as the balloon, a vast bundle of heavy rubberised fabric was laboriously unloaded from the first lorry by four men and dragged across the front garden, uprooting a selection of tea roses. It was then hoisted onto the garage roof with a mighty heave and having cleared that obstacle, (leaving the hand-crafted weathercock facing south,) the great envelope was lowered onto the patio amidst a shower of roof tiles and then dragged over and laid out on the extensive lawn. The men then returned to the second lorry containing the gondola and hauled it, heavy with ropes and cables, over the partially bald garage roof (re-aligning the weathervane to point due north) completing the already partial destruction of a small pergola. They then left through the house leaving a trail of mud on the delicate Bokhara runner in the hall and decapitating a Capodimonte figurine by the front door.

Errol, after observing that the surface of the garage roof resembled the nosecone of a NASA shuttle after an arduous descent to Earth, walked over to the basket and peered into its dark depths. He cleared his throat.

'Spacious,' he said. 'And somewhat *larger* than I'd imagined.'

'It's not a toy,' said Trevor severely, using the confident tone he used to reassure his brother and diminish his own disquiet. 'We'll be thankful for a substantial gondola when we're aloft.'

Errol gulped. For a moment he'd forgotten about the ascent, and would have traded in the basket for a smaller one if it had meant reducing the cruising altitude he feared Trevor had in mind. Concern jostled with distaste as he regarded the vast expanse of material spread out on the grass for it reminded him of a whale's body lying on a beach in Scotland he'd seen as a child, and how *solid* its body had looked in death. The grounded balloon seemed to him to possess a similar weighty appearance and he thoughtfully felt the thin wicker wall of the basket between his thumb and finger.

'How long is all this going to take?' asked Cynthia on cue and Trevor stiffened with the unspoken response that always sprang to his mind hearing the familiar words. Then he reminded himself of her patience in the planning and help with the food – not to mention how reliant they were on her co-operation as ground control. By keeping them in sight she could track their progress from the ground in the Hillman Imp, staying in contact by mobile phone. And when they landed she was to summon the hirers who would retrieve the balloon and basket.

But now it was the morning of the flight and there was much to do. Errol began lugging two heavy propane cylinders from the garage and in his haste tripped over a wire and badly crushed his hand between the cannisters as he fell. He tried alleviating the intense pain through what Trevor referred to as 'brainless capering' among the coiled ropes and hawsers leaving them in a tangled mess. Not until Cynthia had bandaged his hand did Errol regain the composure to pay attention to his brother.

'After we've fed gas into the balloon,' said Trevor. 'We'll just *float* up, light as a feather.'

"Just be careful, the pair of you,' said Cynthia eyeing the propane bottles with concern.

'The heavy lifting's over,' said Errol, nursing his aching hand.

'Only fine tuning needed now,' said Trevor, gamely. 'The lightest touch on the tiller.'

'Just relax, Cynth, and enjoy following the flight,' said Errol, but recalling the outcome of past assurances, she remained silent.

After securing the base of the balloon to the basket, best practice would have tilted the gondola to one side and gently injected heated air from the burners into the great globe. But the brothers, unhindered by theory or experience, attached the propane tanks to the burners immediately below the ringed base of the balloon and turned on the heaters at full blast.

Following some alarming writhings the flabby envelope, accompanied by loud, rude noises billowed up at an alarming rate to form a roughly spherical but unstable shape. This gave Errol the opportunity to attach the 'flying wires,' (vertical tapes sewn into the loops of the fabric) to the basket using carabiners. A fiddly job with two hands at the best of times but almost impossible with his injured hand encased in its fat bandage. Then, as if on cue, a playful breeze sprang up causing the partially inflated balloon to begin swinging, twisting wildly and knotting its harnesses, the ropes and wires joining with the unravelling bandage on Errol's hand by getting in everyone's way.

Mad with pain and exasperation he leapt into the gondola to free the cordage but something was anchoring it to the ground and straining at this invisible mooring it began to tilt. Trevor, returning from the garage with a spare gas cylinder stared open mouthed as Errol, arms flailing, fell backwards inside the basket. Luckily Cynthia had the presence of mind to grab a trailing rope and secure it to a hardy shrub planted in the lawn, but the upward thrust of the billowing balloon was now too powerful even for this sturdy hybrid and began pulling it out of the ground. Trevor, released from his trancelike state, rushed forward and hurled sandbags into the basket until the envelope floated over a more or less stable gondola.

High voltage tension and extreme physical activity often forced Trevor's deep reservoirs of intolerance to the surface, infecting him with manic energy and a temporary loss of sanity. In this state of mind, he leapt into the gondola treading on Errol and shouting out to Cynthia to free the rope. She promptly obeyed while his brother, a little dizzy after being struck by a flying sandbag, struggled to regain his footing. Trevor, ignoring him, unwisely adjusted the burner and a fountain of fire burst upward as more heated air surged into the balloon. He then hurled the last of the sandbags overboard and as they lurched upwards Cynthia fell backwards in alarm. With only seconds to spare she grabbed the large backpack on the lawn beside her, threw into it some keys lying on the ground and hurled both into the gondola.

The gas burners roared away as the super-heated air poured into the balloon and it rose rapidly sheering away to the east. It was several roads away by the time Cynthia had collected her wits and run to the car to find there were no keys in the ignition. She searched frantically in her handbag before recalling that she'd thrown them into the gondola in the backpack. Her stomach lurched, but there was nothing to be done and she watched helplessly as the balloon drifted swiftly away until it was out of sight.

Meanwhile, aloft, Trevor gave a great sigh of relief.

'Free, free at last,' he breathed. 'Slipped from "the surly bonds of earth". What a release! How worthwhile it's all been.'

'Wonderful!' said Errol, getting into the spirit of the thing in spite of pain, slight concussion and his fear of heights. At this elevation he felt his fears were groundless, an odd phrase to come to mind, but excusable after his vicissitudes.

'Now to contact Cynthia,' said Trevor after ten minutes of rapid ascent. 'The backpack, please, Errol.'

His brother, watching the ground receding rapidly beneath them with controlled panic threw over the pack. Trevor fished around inside it and found some plastic containers full of sandwiches, two packets of digestive biscuits and a bunch of keys, which puzzled him.

'No, I meant the other pack,' he shouted. 'The one with the communications stuff in it.'

There was a moment's silence.

'Hurry up,' Trevor shouted, 'I can't spot Cynth. down there in the car and she needs directions.'

'*I* haven't got it,' said Errol, 'I thought you had it. What's in the one you've got there?'

'Sandwiches and a keyring,' said Trevor

'What sort of sandwiches?'

'Does it matter? Tuna.'

'*With* mayo?'

'I don't know. Yes.'

'I *hate* tuna with mayo.' She *knows* that. What sort of a keyring?'

'A bloody car keyring.'

'Why did you bring that? We don't need it up here.'

'I know that dimwit. *We* don't but *she* does because she's Ground Control, remember. And we've got to go down, *now*. Turn off the burner, Errol, turn off the burner.'

'I can't turn the control knob, with my hand like this.'

'Alright I'll do it! Let me do it! It's stuck – pass me a spanner, Errol. Pass me a bloody spanner.'

'It's in the other backpack,' said Errol. 'We left in a hurry... things got... forgotten.'

'Then we'll just have to open the parachute vents at the top of the balloon to let the heated air out, won't we?' said Trevor. 'Make yourself useful for once and pull on the control wire.'

'Where is it?'

'How should I know? The instruction manual's in the other rucksack.'

'I thought you knew all about this thing,' said Errol.

'You always expect me to know everything,' said Trevor. 'What I *do* know is that we can't open the vents, unless someone, possibly the person who should have connected up the control wire in the first place, climbs up and does it manually.'

'I'm not doing that, it's far too dangerous,' said Errol, in terror. 'Do *you* fancy climbing up the side of a balloon this size at this height?'

'You don't want to hear what I fancy doing right now,' said Trevor. 'With you in the starring role.'

'It's not all down to me, you know.'

'The mobile phone's on the ground as well I suppose...'

'Ah…um… yes. Probably. Yes.'

'Errol, let me summarise our current position,' said Trevor. 'We didn't have a flight plan to start with so that's all right, because we knew we couldn't control where we were going. But we do need to tell ground control by phone, where we're heading, especially when we're out of sight. But we can't because we haven't got a phone. But not to worry, Cynthia couldn't follow us in the car anyway, because we've got her car keys. Now we can't stop going up because the burner controls are stuck, and we've no tools to free them. And we can't open the release vents to let the hot air out because we haven't attached the wire to operate them. A good start, Errol.'

'And we've got tuna sandwiches *with* mayo which I *hate.*'

★ ★ ★

The balloon continued rising and although it became cold it was beautiful up there. After some time and even with the gas exhausted the balloon remained buoyant enough to pick up a strong north-easterly wind, and they passed over the English coastline and continued north-north-east over the Netherlands drifting towards the Baltic. Over Kaliningrad Oblast, the Russian enclave between Poland and Lithuania, they entered Soviet airspace creating consternation on the ground and several Russian jets were scrambled.

'They're only curious,' said Trevor. 'If they mean to threaten us they'll show us the rockets under their wings.'

'What should we do if they do that?' muttered Errol. 'Wave some tupper-ware sandwich boxes at them?'

Trevor treated the remark with distain but would have been intrigued to learn that they had indeed become the focus of diplomatic exchanges at an international level with the Russians accusing them of being a new "terror weapon". And as news of their flight leaked out from Cynthia's frantic calls to the balloon hirers, helicopters, micro lights, small planes and even a flock of highflying cranes took a passing interest in them.

To spare them embarrassment, Cynthia, after being towed home by a local garage and aware that their flightpath was unplanned, felt obliged to withhold details of their ultimate destination. But suggestions on the best way of terminating their flight were abandoned when the only effective solutions, largely from members of the US gun lobby chapter in the UK would have entailed serious risk to the balloonists. Thus, their destination remained a mystery to the watching world for three whole days for the wind had dropped, until the honour fell on Estonia the most northerly of the Baltic states.

The actual landing site was Muuga aedlinn, a rural location with few paved streets, but when news reached the capital, nearby Tallinn, arrangements were made to transport the now famous deflated balloon and its occupants on horse drawn waggons, gaily decorated with seasonal flowers along country lanes thronged by cheering countryfolk.

In Tallinn's centre is a charming square and it was here, to great acclaim and much rejoicing that the balloon, still the object of intense international interest, found its final resting place. And in a hastily conceived but lavish ceremony some days later Trevor and Errol were invested as Freemen of the City and the balloon was purchased by the City Fathers to become a popular tourist attraction.

Once home the pair enjoyed a few days of the popular acclaim awarded to temporary celebrities in a news-parched summer but, in spite of lucrative offers, they never took to the skies again. Indeed, it is said that, for a short while afterwards Trevor almost lost his enthusiasm for adventure altogether. And although his brother's injuries healed rapidly and his fear of heights vanished for ever, what he could never banish from his mind was something quite different.

For the privations of the journey had elevated in Errol something from mild aversion and mere repulsion to an implacable hatred. And for the rest of his life, he possessed an irrational dislike not only for the innocents he saw devouring tuna sandwiches, but even more for their blameless fellow consumers whose skipjack was embellished "with Mayo." For them he reserved a particularly hot spot in a very unpleasant hell that he spent many happy hours devising.

A VIEW of the BAY

W here the River Somme and five other rivers meet to join the English Channel they create a vast bay. Walking on the limitless sands of this place of cloud-swept lightness, it seems that here gravity has surrendered its iron grip on matter and space and every season strengthens the feeling.

In spring flurries of wind whip over the sandy levels bringing the salt taste of the sea to the marshes and pebble banks, home to samphire and delicate glasswort. Fluttering flocks of small brown birds skim over the whispering sedge fields beneath the busy wings of larks, and tiny, tough flowers start to bloom beside the sturdy sea-lavender like little bright stars, yellow and white. Cattails and rushes are astir and all is bustle as the busy sedge wren, its tail held high, bounces around full of life. And now the brown, bruised winter grass is transformed into channels of bright green, sprinkled with daisies and dandelions.

In summer the burning sun in the cloudless sky scorches sedge and sand, too hot now for human feet, and a film of shimmering air over the tidal flats blends the border between land and sea on the far-off shore. Songbird and snake now sleep the heat away, deep in sedge-high shade or dark burrow, while above, white storks float high on draughts of air as if lulled by the dream-like drumming of the waves on the distant strand. And sometimes there's a hint of spicy fragrance in the air as if you were in Provence or the Camargue watching filmy herds of horses floating through the quivering heat.

In autumn the sun's dominance yields to the wind and rain for this is now the realm of the westerlies and the flatland offers no hindrance to the gales that sweep in from the open sea. Gone now are airless summer days replaced by the lonely howl of the wind gusting over the billowing sheets of waving, soaking sedge-grass. And spring's once bright blooms lie withered on rotted stalks while hardy succulents grip the soil tightly beneath noisy waves of birds leaving for winter quarters. Now days darken under sullen skies and everywhere green is fast leaving the land.

The year hastens on, and winter life becomes harder for those huddling in houses around the margins of the bay. Few visitors now frequent the bay's salt-flats or the sedge-ponds, even to see the sublime sunsets or when a heavy frost makes the air sparkle and dead twigs crackle underfoot. Ownership has now passed to the natural residents: the geese and the waders, the water rats and the rabbits each with its own habitat and no desire to share it with humans.

There will always be special people who love places like this whatever the weather or season and leaving them behind for ever is agony for them. One such was Joan of Arc who crossed this bay in a boat long ago after her capture by the English on her way to trial and a terrible death. She must have guessed at her fate and looked with fierce longing at the great open space under the dear French sky, where birds flew unfettered high above her native land.

Perhaps the image of the bay remained with her until the very end, when she desperately needed all her courage and strength. Those who treasure such places must surely trust it did and love them all the more for that.

THE LOST
CONNECTION

In summer it's hard work pushing through the sweaty, heaving crowds on the border with Mexico seven miles south of Yuma, Arizona where July temperatures average 42 centigrade. But you can leave all this frantic bustle behind if you go south, towards the Gulf of California, set in its world of intense heat, fierce winds and maddening flies.

Driving through the parched rocky terrain, white dust whirling in your wake it's 150 miles to reach the Gulf whose cool, dark, wave flecked waters look inviting but somehow forbidding. It's a vast body of water, 3,000 metres deep in places and 900 miles long, world renowned for whale spotting and containing nearly a thousand islands most of them so small you'd regard them as large rocks. A very few of the larger ones are inhabited and won't look very remote on a large scale map as the modern city of La Paz is only a hundred miles to the south.

Marieanne, a modern Californian, avid for new experience and keen on "authenticity" has chosen an island in the Gulf where she plans to spend time living among Mexican fisherfolk. At first blush the place seems attractive for it's uncrowded, the sunsets are to die for and the fishing's said to be good. But although sheltered from most of the northerly gales that sweep down in winter, powerful winds can swirl around it at any time of the year.

A friend knows someone who runs a boat taking tourists along the coast whale watching and he knows the island and its people. He's fixed her up with somewhere to stay and from the grainy photos she's seen it looks really *valid*. Fish will be good for her diet and yoga will sustain her in the solitude she craves in moments of stress. Long healing silences can be punctuated by meaningful conversations in schoolgirl Spanish with real, uncomplicated people. The wine should be drinkable and the Wi-Fi link adequate.

The day her boat arrives there's a heavy sea running and as usual at that time of year the wind's gusting fiercely from the north. Only a very good skipper would undertake the passage across to the island, but he manages it in worsening weather. She's deposited hastily with her huge backpack onto a battered jetty half submerged by flying spray while the boat swiftly turns to plough back through the heavy swell.

She's a feisty person, well-nourished and valued from birth, fit and youngish. And it's just as well for there's no one under seventy-five there to help carry her luggage up the steep ramp running from the jetty to a tumbledown shelter. It's here the islanders salt the fish they catch using a great table, thick as a butcher's block, its surface black with congealed blood. Sickly cats gnaw frantically at the piles of entrails scattered beneath it before giving the rats a chance to feast on the glistening offal. The wind keeps the flies away but when it drops they resume buzzing and fighting to feast and lay eggs and then a sickening stench greets Marieanne's nostrils. She struggles along with her luggage and meets her host Jose, eighty-two years old, weather beaten and half blind with untreated cataracts. His rough hands shake as he reaches out to welcome her but he makes no attempt to take her heavy luggage. An old woman in black clothes, almost bent double and virtually toothless mumbles something to her in strange Spanish and points to a hovel higher up the hill.

Marieanne has toughed it out in India and is drinking it all in, trying hard to forget her nausea from the crossing and the horror of the salting area. To her slight dismay her accommodation is not as sheltered from the wind as she would have chosen but at least it's got a corrugated iron roof. She notices that the walls of adobe brick are crumbling, especially around the windows where the dirty thick plastic sheeting, in lieu of glass, has come adrift in places. There's a straw mattress on the floor of the single room and a small table with a broken chair. Asking about a bathroom she's pointed to a tiny concrete shed some way down the hill with a sheet of corrugated iron propped on the wall making do for a door. Inside she sees a hole in the ground surrounded by soiled planks and a rusty pail half full of dirty water placed nearby. It smells dreadful.

Such is her introduction to an island no more than two hour's drive to an ultra modern marina along a motorway on the opposite western shore. And here she experiences life on the real edge and not the comfortable austerity of a middle-class Indian retreat.

She's surprised to find that water is simply the most precious thing that humans possess although much taken for granted and therefore least valued by hygiene-obsessed Californians. There's no fresh water on the island with its sparse rainfall and no shower or WC. Water for cooking is greedily husbanded and has to be brought from the mainland in huge plastic containers which must be paid for. The only income the occupants have is from the fish they catch and cure and the few remaining men spend long hours fishing in all weathers with the women slaving away at salting what they catch. To make matters worse there's no guarantee of regular supplies, for the heavy seas often prevent vessels making it to the jetty.

This leads to a severe shortage of the most basic types of food and even fruit is a luxury. And it's on this meagre, insufficient diet that the old men and women carry out their back breaking toil. If their clothes become worn they darn them; if their roof lets in the rain they beg the ships that visit for plastic to patch over the holes; and if they get really sick and the seas are running high, they die.

Once there'd been a half-hearted attempt from the mainland local government to install a water desalination plant on the island and footings had been built. But after the top town officials received their official Mercedes there were no funds to finish the job and now all that remains is rust-marked, crumbling concrete. Nor is there any Wi-Fi connection – only a battered radio transmitter which none of the islanders know how use properly or fix when it fails. It's lain unused for months.

After a week Marieanne develops severe diarrhea, becomes feverish and runs a high temperature. The weather worsens and because no boat can reach them the water nearly runs out. Then the unthinkable happens and her world collapses around her. Her determination not to use an i-phone didn't prevent her bringing one and now, driven by despair, when she tries to use it she finds the batteries dead. And that means real isolation, for the phone is literally her lifeline. Not only as a means of getting help but also an echo chamber of her voice where like-minded contacts endlessly endorse the validity of her views and feelings.

It's the final straw and, weeping and moaning, she rocks backwards and forwards on the filthy floor of her room, working herself up until she hyperventilates. When she recovers, she rages at the *unfairness* of things and then a terrible anger rises up in her and she blunders out of the room and rushes down to where the old couple are gutting fish.

'What's the matter with you fucking people?' she screams at them. They look up, surprised and shocked.

'Why do you live like this in this stinking, shitty mess with no fucking Wi-Fi you fucking, filthy peasants,' she screams. 'Why, why, why?'

They don't understand and the old lady, white-faced and trembling now at the onslaught, begins to cry softly like a small, wounded animal, muttering in Spanish. She's had more sorrow and loss in her life than Marieanne has ever known or probably ever will know and has survived the death of two husbands and six children with desperate dignity and quiet strength. She is bewildered at the hysteria and loss of control from one so young the cause of which, if explained to her, would be far beyond her comprehension. Her frail husband moves clumsily to her side putting a blood-soaked, shaking arm around her and they stare in wonder at the swearing, raging, wild-eyed woman. '*What have we done*? they seem to say.

'Oh never fucking, mind!' Marieanne snarls and runs back to her room where she throws herself on her bed and the phone onto the floor. Soon afterwards she collapses, and the old folk do everything they can for her. Although water is now critically low the woman constantly bathes her forehead with the precious liquid rather than drink it herself. She doesn't complain, for hardship and sacrifice get easier with decades of practice. With them looking after her day and night for a week, Marieanne hangs on and when the weather clears a boat gets in. The crew carry her from her befouled room down to the jetty where the vessel is lying a way off in the surging waves to avoid crashing into the harbour wall.

Moaning softly on a makeshift stretcher, her face drained of colour and her long blonde hair matted and plastered, Marieanne looks truly dreadful. The old lady regards this poor, shallow shell of a person with pity and compassion and goes to find and then return with a few of the precious shells she sells for a pittance to the rare tourists who visit her island. She's chosen some of the prettiest and presses a few into the American's hand.

When Marieanne reaches the mainland her insurance cover ensures she gets the best treatment in a modern hospital before flying back to California. Reflecting on her ordeal she recalls reading that civilized man is only seven meals away from being a savage and had often thought that her less adventurous friends might be only two showers and a chardonnay away from such a fate. She'd always felt *different* although a witness of her reaction to her loss of a phone might have found that fanciful.

Healthy, varied food and a disciplined use of alcohol soon have the roses back in her cheeks and before long her spiritually nourished life is resumed. She now feels enriched by the suffering she's undergone, although her thoughts seldom stray from her own distress. She's only a hazy recollection of the gentle people on the island with so little who helped her so much when she needed them most.

And then, one day, in her backpack she finds the delicate shells given to her by the old woman and a dim memory stirs producing a vague feeling of guilt. That makes her feel uncomfortable and she seeks out Linette, her mental-health therapist and influencer with whom she shares her distress.

'Oh Marieanne,' says Linette in mock despair, smiling down at her on the tanning table in the gym complex where they meet. 'What have we lost sight of?'

For a moment Marieanne is silent, worried that she is referring to some problem with her skin-care treatment.

'And what have we forgotten?' persists her therapist.

'I don't know,' she says, weakly. 'What?'

'Team "Me", that's what,' says Linette, a touch impatiently.

'Oh,' says Marianne.

'Warm-heart, don't you think that feeling guilty is a bit like taking an unnecessary hit for the Team?' says Linette.

'I suppose...' said Marieanne.

'Who did we agree are on your Team?'

'I forget.'

'"Pleasure, Pride and Empowerment," no guilt there,' says Linette triumphantly, and Marieanne nods her agreement.

Having established that such thoughts impede the search for wellness to which she is committed she throws away the shells as an unhelpful reminder of such an ugly, life-denying experience.

And now she has to counter a wistfulness about giving up such pretty things and this becomes a persistent anguish.

'Valid feelings,' Linette assures her. 'But they relate only to a loss of fleeting pleasure the satisfaction of which would have only hampered your journey towards true happiness.'

Comforted by that thought, Marieanne returns to her personal "journey" on that desolate island, not averse to sharing an edited account of that terrible time with others on social media and never denying any implication that it was only her fortitude that sustained her through its darkest moments.

This resonates so well with many others suffering existential pain, that she's advised, if properly handled, her future could be very bright. For it might embrace not only the consistent devotion of her current admirers but also the affection of many new fans leading to a well-earned celebrity for many years to come.

RITES AND
WRONGS

'Grosspapa,' said little Flurina, standing on one leg and looking up at him in the big armchair. 'Do you know what my name means?'

'Yes, darling girl,' the old gentleman smiled, putting down his newspaper.

'Is it nice?' she said, twisting round and looking at him closely.

'Very nice,' he said. 'Your mummy and I chose it very, very carefully. It means "flower" and they are beautiful in Switzerland in the Spring.'

'Is our country *very* beautiful,' she said.

'Yes,' he laughed.

'Because of the flowers?'

'Not just that, darling, but think of all our lovely trees as well.'

'My teacher said we must all plant trees to make the whole Earth good,' she said.

'And she's right to say that. It's the correct thing to do,' he said, beaming down at her.

'Grosspapa,' said Flurina. 'Are there many old gentlemen like you, living here in Kirchenfeld in big houses with people to look after them.'

'Not so very many,' he said, proud of living in Berne's most prestigious neighbourhood. 'Why do you ask?'

'Because teacher says many old gentlemen living in big houses here belong to something with a very long name. It's like "burgosie" but longer.'

'Ah, she means the Bourgeoisie de Berne,' he said. 'A very old club and it's a great honour to belong to it. What did she say about it?'

'She said it was old fashioned and the gentlemen were allowed to do things that weren't right.'

'Such as?' he said, with an edge to his voice.

'Like having the right to cut down a tree every year. All of you. You do too, 'cos I've seen the logs.'

'Ah yes – the ones we love to burn at Christmas time.'

'But Grosspapa,' said Flurina, 'I'd rather have the tree.'

'It's a very respected and ancient rite.'

'But is it right proper?' she said. 'Proper right to kill a tree and just burn it all away?'

'I think it's teatime, darling,' he said gently, picking up his newspaper. But the smile had disappeared.

DAMNED BY THE BELL

*Occam's razor: an explanation for an event which, using the fewest
assumptions, is usually correct.*

If you're looking for evidence of modern miracles in Italy the
formerly remote villages in the Ligurian landscape would be
a good place to start. It's hilly country north of the busy city
of La Spezia and, half-way between Pisa and Genoa on the west
coast, are the Cinque Terre, the famous fishing villages at one
time accessible only by boat. And it was in a hotel in one of
these places called Vernazza that my wife Lucy and I met Doctor
Olivera, with whom we discussed many things, among which
was the subject of divine intervention

We were there looking for material for a travel book we were
writing and the retired doctor who lived alone in Florence was
a fellow guest at our hotel. He'd been a local family practitioner
for many years and was happy to tell us about the life and
traditions of the villagers amongst whom he'd spent much of his
professional life. That sounded like gold dust to us to give our
book a more "authentic" feel.

'People living their whole lives in remote Italian villages are
often very superstitious,' the doctor said. 'And although deeply
suspicious of strangers they can be gullible to those they trust.

They like a good story and but just *love* a good miracle! Would you like to hear a story to illustrate what I mean?'

'Indeed we would, Signor Dottore,' we said. 'And perhaps we might share a bottle of Prima Terra Cerico with you, while we listen.'

He brightened up at that, and with the glasses filled we sat back and listened.

'It happened in a village up the coast from here towards Porto Fino,' he began. 'A powerful stream flows through it from high in the hills and the water, rushing past an old waterwheel, plummets through a narrowing between high rocky banks before plunging down to the beach. And high above all this turmoil on a rocky promontory loom the silent ruins of an ancient abbey.'

'Sounds a fearsome place,' said Lucy.

'And dangerous, too,' said the doctor. 'There's a meadow overlooking the stream where families gather for picnics in summer and the adults are always wary of letting their children wander near the stream. The narrow path beside the water, is often wet from the spray and if you slipped and fell into the stream your body would immediately go into deep shock in the icy cold water. After that more than one walker has ended up with their body tangled among the dank weeds on the rotting paddles of the waterwheel!'

'Mountain-fed water can be freezing on the hottest days,' we agreed.

'It was a late afternoon in early summer not long after I'd retired and I was walking along the path,' continued the doctor. 'Seeing a commotion in the water I thought some animal had fallen in but seeing arms frantically thrashing in the water, I screamed for help. Some young men from a family picnicking on the meadow heard me, rushed down and pulled a young man from the stream. We laid him face down and began pumping the water out of him with until with a great gasp he began breathing.'

'Was he in very bad shape?' asked my wife.

'At first there was only the faintest pulse,' said the doctor. 'And with his ashen face and hair plastered down on his scalp he looked terrible. His whole body was just a limp bundle of soaked clothing'

'Did you recognise him?'

'Not at first,' said Olivera. 'But I had this feeling I'd seen him before and then the paramedics arrived, and he was transferred to the nearest hospital.'

'Did anything about him come to mind later?' Lucy asked.

'Nothing special, except this feeling that he was *familiar*,' he said. 'Family doctors like me, operating for years over a large rural area see so many people but he interested me enough to speak to the medic who examined him after he was brought in. He told me it was an odd case, for in his experience someone like him, weak and ill-nourished, struggling alone in that powerful current should have succumbed. But somehow, miraculously, he survived.

'What happened next?'

'He wasn't my patient,' said Olivera. 'But I asked to be kept informed of his progress and they told me that as he was without friends or family, he would be offered counselling. And as I'd helped other people recover from similar traumas they accepted my offer of help.'

'Doubly lucky for him you were around,' said Lucy.

'Perhaps,' he said, enigmatically. 'We met in the room attached to the hospital used for such interviews and as I sat waiting for him to arrive, I couldn't help wondering what had made him seem so familiar.'

At this point the doctor glanced at his empty glass and asked if he was boring us. We assured him he was not and taking the hint, we ordered another bottle and urged him to continue.

'As you might expect he was still very weak,' he said. 'And rather *crushed,* not unusual in failed suicide cases. I judged him to be in his late twenties, thin, clean shaven with alert eyes and dressed in ill-fitting clothing which had clearly come from a charity shop. It was then I recognised him as a professional beggar who did the rounds of the local villages and was often in trouble with police for soliciting money from tourists. His name, I learned, was Marcus.'

'I'm Doctor Olivera,' I said. 'I spotted you in the river, but I'm afraid I couldn't help get you out of the water. I'm not as young as I was.'

He gave me a thin smile and mumbled his thanks, looking down at his feet.

'His life as a vagrant was the usual story that preceded a suicide attempt,' the doctor continued. 'Job loss through illness, love affair gone sour, lack of money and living hand to mouth in doss houses and hostels for the homeless. And, although he was not very well educated, I found him articulate, intelligent and perceptive but also suspected he could be *persuasive* although some might have thought the word "streetwise" would describe him rather better.'

'Did you find out what had led him to such a desperate act?' I asked.

'With these cases I'd found it helpful not to dwell on the past but to move on,' said Olivera. 'We found him a job stacking shelves in a supermarket and a regular bed in a clean hostel of which I was a trustee. I was pleased to see his health and appearance improving, but always, at the back of my mind, was the enigma of his survival.'

'Did the other doctors feel like that?' I asked.

'Yes, they were puzzled as well,' he said. 'So when I got to know him better I asked him what he remembered about his struggle in the water.'

'What makes you ask that?' he said, suddenly wary.

'I wondered what made you want to cling on to life in such a desperate situation.'

'If we go and see where it happened,' he said. 'It might help us both discover what happened.'

24

'Was the village far from the clinic?'

'An hour's drive,' said the doctor. 'We started early and there was no one there when we arrived but, in spite of the bright sunshine, there was an inescapably *brooding* quality about the place. The water hissed and frothed in the stream and with the dark mass of the abbey ruins above it looked dank and dismal. "*An ideal place for a depressed person to take the final plunge*" I thought.'

'I've come back here many times, Doc,' said Marcus. 'To try to understand what happened.'

'Where now?' I asked, looking around, and he told me to follow him.

He led the way up some steep weathered steps leading to the abbey ruins and at the top we went through a gaping hole into a large hall whose walls were stripped of plaster exposing crumbling brickwork. We stumbled on beneath a ruined roof through rubble amid smells of damp and decay.

'Come on,' Marcus said, and we clambered even higher up a narrow keystone twist of steps to a small tower from which you could look down onto the surging water far below.

'We were in what had once been a bell tower,' said Olivera. 'You could still see the rotted remains of the wooden beam and the "headstock," that had supported the heavy bells.'

'For most of my life I was a strict Roman Catholic,' Marcus said, 'But then I relapsed. But when I was almost at my last gasp I heard a bell tolling, and my lost faith returned, filling my soul and strengthening my body.'

'So the sound was a *warning* to you as a Catholic, not to commit an unforgivable sin.'

'I supposed so – but can you see a bell here?' said Marcus.

'It must have been another one you heard.'

'There's nothing near here, believe me.'

'So, what do you make of it?'

'Obviously it was a *sign* from heaven,' he said. 'A miraculous sign.'

'Did anyone else hear the bell?' I asked.

'I was told an old villager heard something tolling at exactly the same time I was in the water,' he said. 'And his relatives said it sounded to him like the old Abbey funeral bell he remembered when he was a lad.'

'What happened to him?'

'He died soon after that very night,' he said. 'And I'm sure, although the bell meant we were both to die, I was saved for some reason. I don't yet know why, but I just *know* it.'

'I suspect that the church is very critical of such interventions,' I said. 'It's more likely to be coincidental with the old man dying when he did than a miracle Just be glad that you survived.'

★ ★ ★

The old doctor knew how to spin out a good story and he smiled at us, sipping his wine.

'Well, go on,' said Lucy.

'After our meeting the next morning Marcus was gone,' he said. 'He just disappeared into thin air.'

'Ah,' Lucy said. 'I didn't see that coming.'

'But word had got around somehow, about the bell, and as you might imagine some villagers claimed they'd heard it that night.'

'Superstition breeding suggestion?' I asked.

'Is that all you make of his experience?' said Olivera, taking a sip of wine.

'I prefer the simplest explanation for such things and that rules out miracles.'

'I agree, it's possible he *thought* he heard the bell,' said Lucy. 'And because of the guilt and remorse about what he was doing it gave him the strength to survive.'

'So, Occam's razor, it is,' said Olivera, with a smile.

'There's more, isn't there doctor?' said my wife.

'Some years later I returned to the area,' he said. 'And I was taking a digestif in the shade outside a café in Manarola, one of the smallest of these villages in the Cinque Terre, when Marcus walked past. I couldn't believe my eyes. He still looked scruffy but had a bit of a *swagger* about him.'

'Hello doc,' he said, when I called out to him. 'Good to see you.'

'I thought you were dead.'

'Alive and kicking,' he laughed.

'I invited him to join me for a drink and we sat relaxing in that sleepy, midday calm you get in remote villages where the men have been out all night fishing and the women have been up since dawn.'

'What's happened to you since we last met?' I asked.

'Oh, I just pushed off and laid low for a bit,' he said. 'Thinking up a plan for the future.'

'Any more thoughts about your miraculous escape from the stream?'

'Oh that,' he laughed. 'No mystery there. I was often high on drugs those days and sleeping behind the rocks by the river. Suddenly I woke up and still half asleep wandered towards the river, missed my footing, slipped and fell in. It was the shock of the cold water that brought me to my senses, I didn't want to drown, now did I?'

'So you fooled us into thinking it was a suicide attempt?'

'No I didn't,' he said. '*You* fooled yourselves. I never said I was attempting suicide. Not once.'

'What about the bell? The so-called "miracle".'

'I made that bit up,' he said. 'As I was coming to, I heard one of the men who saved me say, "It's a miracle he's still alive".' While I was away I thought a lot about that. When I heard about the old peasant dying I guessed the sound of a bell was only in his mind. But then I thought if I said I'd heard it too but had been saved for a purpose, it would sound pretty miraculous.

Sorry doc, but I tried it out first on you, taking you round the ruins like that.'

'I was very put out when he said that!' Olivera laughed.

'What did he do then?'

'When he reappeared, he told the villagers he'd been on a "retreat" to work out what the "miracle" meant and then he started "working" the villages as he put it.'

'Once a beggar, you know...' he said. 'And saved by the bell was my line. I found it worked like a charm! I give them God's blessing and they give me money and I've made a very good living.'

'I'm surprised you got away with it,' I said. 'They're a tough bunch these villagers.'

'They were suspicious at first,' said Marcus. 'But, by God they *so* love a good miracle. And look at me now – I'm a local saint. Touched by God, like Maradona's hand.'

'I was speechless,' said Olivera.

'I'm not surprised,' said Lucy.

'Then he said something was worrying him and I asked him what it was.'

'If they're ill and I give them my blessing they always get better,' he said. '*Always.* Even those really sick. I'm really scared. What's going on, doc? Tell me it's not a miracle!'

Doctor Olivera, paused to take a sip of wine, smiled at us, and said, 'So what would you have done if you were me?'

'I would have spoken to the local doctors about it and told him the truth,' Lucy suggested. 'And then you could tell him that his so-called miracle was a fairy tale.'

'So did you check out his story?'

'Yes, and it was quite true,'said Olivera. 'The medics were as baffled as he was, and I told him as much.'

'How did he take that?'

'He seemed resigned, shrugged his shoulders and walked away without a word. I sometimes wish I hadn't let him go so easily.'

'Why, what happened?'

'Now he felt he really possessed what he claimed he already had,' said Olivera. 'He couldn't handle it. He wasn't cut out to be a saint, for like most of us he was born to be a sinner and happy with his lot. And if he really had a "miraculous escape" for a divine purpose, the burden of sanctity weighed heavily on him.'

'What happened then?'

'He went back to the river that night,' said the doctor. 'And this time he made sure he wasn't coming back. He'd been in the water for hours when they found his body.'

'Did anyone hear a bell tolling about the time he went into the water?' I asked, on a sudden hunch.

'No idea,' said Doctor Olivera.

'You mean you didn't even try to find out?' said Lucy.

'My dear,' he said, taking a sip of wine. 'I've seen so many inexplicable things in my life that now I'm old I don't search for explanations. Sometimes it's best to leave things untouched. We Italians do relish a good mystery you know – but not as much as we love a real miracle!'

WHAT GOES AROUND COMES AROUND

'd been abroad for many years but had reached the age when not a day passed without my thinking about death and I decided it was time to come home to England.

In my long years in Australia and New Zealand I was no longer in touch with the literary world which at one point had completely dominated my life. I was a professional journalist plugging away at novels and short stories in my spare time. I enjoyed writing fiction and although my plots were rather over complicated my characterisation was good. The early books had a following and sold quite well but I decided to give up writing. I retrained as a lawyer and emigrated to Australia, raised a family, saw them grow up and go their own way and lost a dear wife after forty years of happy marriage.

Now I planned to live out my days in London in a modest flat in Bayswater with the few acquaintances I had left. My long absence abroad had told on former friendships which had ended like so many do either unaccountably or through natural wastage.

But I had a good memory for the past and was interested one day to see there was to be a book signing in a famous bookshop in Piccadilly. And to my surprise, the author had been a close friend of mine in the distant past but now just a name.

I attended the event and made myself known to Leslie Knowles the "well known author." It seemed he'd been a best seller over many years and I recalled our work writing together when we were very young. He must have greatly improved his skills for, in all modesty, I was the better writer. But I held no grudge, and welcomed his success.

When I introduced myself, his face went from puzzled to wary recognition, pleasure and then despair.

'I knew we would meet again one day,' he said. 'And I've *dreaded* it.'

'Really?'

'I'm a rich and famous writer now,' he said, sorrowfully. 'And all because of you. I just don't know how to face you after all this time.'

'Explain,' I said.

'My first book was a lift from the last unpublished manuscript you lent me,' he said. 'And when I said I didn't like it you said to get rid of it. Actually I thought it was very good and when you'd gone away it was virtually the manuscript I published as a novel. I never looked back and you haven't made a penny out of it. And it's too late now.'

'So what,' I said. 'Water under the bridge.'

'Then I went back over some of the other things you'd sent me in manuscript when we exchanged ideas and drafts, and used those as well, and those made my name.'

'Mate, you've had to live with this all your life,' I said. 'Isn't that enough punishment.'

'No,' he said.

We parted then and never saw each other again. At first I felt genuinely sorry for him, for I know how hard it is to forgive yourself for someone you've wronged. But then I felt angrier with him than I'd thought possible, because the manuscripts he borrowed from me I was editing for someone called Peter Thorne. And it was *his* plots I took and then his wife, and in return Peter took his life. It was then I gave up writing.

Now that cheating pommy bastard of a writer Leslie Knowles has brought all that up again and *I've* got to live with all that locked away self-reproach and remorse festering inside me again. At my age! And with only this story to show for it in the few years I've got left before I die, guilty, unloved and unmourned.

THE DECANTER

xperience had taught my wife Ann and I that hotel publicity is usually deceptive but if you know what you're looking for you can spot the good and avoid the bad. On that basis Little Barton House seemed ideal with a cuisine of proven quality and a professional website suggesting it was well run, traditional, slightly formal and childfree. And it had an excellent wine list.

We decided to give it a go and one afternoon in late November drove off the busy main road on the Dorset and Somerset border south of Yeovil and followed the signs to the hotel. The road narrowed before plunging into an unexpectedly deep canyon like Alice disappearing down her hole and emerging, not in Wonderland but in the ancient village of Weston Lamprey with its twelfth-century church built of local Ham stone, famous for the secular carvings on its pew ends. We then took a sharp left turn ascended a steep, metalled track past the Georgian façade of a large farmhouse and drove through the pillared entrance to the hotel grounds.

Dense laurel bushes formed high banks of dark green flanking the winding drive which eventually curved away to give us our first view of the house. True to the publicity it was an elegant Georgian building with lovely low windows and stone steps leading to a modest front door beneath a small portico. There were a few tables and chairs arranged on a small area of gravel in front of the house overlooking a broad flight of steps leading to the lower garden and the trees beyond. And what trees! Giant cedars dwarfing the house and nestling in a steep-sided, densely wooded bowl of juniper, spruce and yew.

We knew that the hotel had only eight bedrooms and we seemed to be the first to arrive for the carpark was empty. We unloaded our luggage, climbed the stone steps to the open front door and stepped into a short, carpeted hallway leading to a small reception desk. No one seemed to be about, but we knew we'd come at a time when staff in small hotels usually take a short break.

It seemed to be our sort of place like a good French *restaurant avec chambres* where the emphasis is on the cooking and wine and not over-fussy designer interiors. To our right was a sitting room with a sulky log fire, comfortable loose-covered settees and deep armchairs on a faded Turkish carpet. And across the hall the dining room looked reassuringly elegant with good spacing between the small tables, each covered with a crisp linen cloth upon which bright cutlery was neatly laid out.

Martina from Slovakia appeared from the room behind the reception desk and welcomed us. Neatly dressed, she had good English, a ready smile and dealt with our registration efficiently. After the signing in we followed her up two flights of stairs to our room which was slightly shabby with an uneven floor and old but not antique furniture. The bathroom was reasonably modern, although we noticed a mass of flies buzzing around the bedroom windows as if it had not been occupied for some time. Nothing seemed seriously amiss except for the flies and Martina dealt so deftly with those that we suspected it was not the first time she'd had to remove their predecessors.

We went down to the empty sitting room for afternoon tea and sat in front of the fire, eating home-baked cakes with a good choice of teas. Afterwards, as it was still light, we strolled down to the lower garden which gave us a good view of the hotel. Hearing the crunch of gravel, we saw a Land Rover sweeping into the car park from which an eye-catching couple emerged. We judged them to be in their sixties, the woman exceedingly plump with a beautiful face whilst the man had a remarkable head of silver hair, which on closer inspection was not home-grown. They left their bags at the foot of the front steps and when they came out disappeared into a small cottage adjoining the front of the hotel. Clearly familiar with the hotel they seemed very much at home.

We continued walking around the grounds and when we turned back towards the house we heard the comforting clink of cutlery on china and saw the new arrivals taking tea on one of the outside tables. We smiled and they introduced themselves as Hugh and Mary. They'd stayed in the hotel many times over the years and thoroughly recommended the cuisine but cautioned us about the woman owner's manner.

'She's not exactly rude,' said Mary. '*Dismissive* perhaps, but she runs a tight ship.'

'She likes things to be just so,' said Hugh.

'What about the chef, her husband?' I asked. 'His food has an excellent reputation.'

'Do you know,' said Mary. 'In all the times we've been here we've hardly ever spoken to him. He seems very shy and usually stays in the kitchen.'

★ ★ ★

We'd booked to eat at eight and came down in good time for a pre-dinner drink, mildly surprised to find ourselves alone in the sitting room. Judging from the hum of conversation in the dining room it seemed the other guests had gone straight into dinner. Martina, now more formally dressed, served us a Chablis and I ordered a good Burgundy to go with dinner. The food was well-served, attractively presented and delicious and the decanted wine at the right temperature tasted superb. Only one thing jarred – amid the sparkling glassware and shining cutlery our decanter looked rather old and distressed. Glancing around I saw similar decanters on the other tables so we guessed they were a "signature" feature of the hotel.

'Don't make a fuss,' my wife said. 'The wine tastes fine to me.'

We took our coffee in an empty sitting-room, and I remarked that the other guests seemed rather unsociable.

'I agree, but I liked the ambiance of the dining room,' replied Ann, who'd been sitting with her back to the wall. 'It's bigger than I thought at first – there's an extension behind some thin curtains on the right as you come in and beyond that there's a conservatory with a table laid up for dinner.'

* * *

After a good night's sleep, the dining room where we took breakfast looked fresh and bright in the morning sunshine. We were enjoying being there and the food was excellent. I said as much to Sarah the owner when she came over to our table, but she dismissed my comment with a short, humourless laugh.

I looked at her more closely, surprised by how much her youthful figure and supple movements had misled me about her age, which I put at around sixty. The cold eyes so knowing in that unlined face betrayed something unspoken giving her a slightly forbidding air. But she seemed interested in our plans for the day and later we learned that the restaurant provided lunch for well-heeled locals and she probably wanted to know who'd be around in the day. And that also explained why our room had been serviced so quickly after breakfast.

'Is the gorge leading to the village natural or man-made?' I asked.

'In the nineteenth century,' she said. 'Lord Ames, whose seat was Barton Grange, so hated seeing trades people that he employed an army of labourers to dig it out of the hill above the village to use when they were delivering goods to his house and this one.'

'Does the family still live there?' said Ann.

'After the Second World War there were deaths, disagreements and tax liabilities and most of the family moved away,' said Sarah. 'Lord Ames lived alone there until illness forced him to move here after his mother died. And when he died no one wanted the place and it was left to rot.'

'Where is it, exactly?' I asked.

'On top of the hill, what's left of it,' she said, pointing. 'But nobody ever goes there.'

She clearly wanted to move on, and we had no wish to keep her talking. As the weather was uncertain, we drove at once to the coast and after lunch in Weymouth took the coast road past Chesil Bank ending up in West Bay. Then, as black clouds were gathering, we drove back earlier than planned to find late lunch guests having brandies in the sitting room. The rain had begun in earnest, and we stayed in our room which became stuffy and gloomy.

'It's getting depressing in here,' said Ann, after a couple of hours. 'The rain's easing so let's get out for a breath of air before it gets too dark.'

I agreed and after picking up my rucksack and our umbrellas from the car we walked up the drive between the banks of dripping laurels and took the steep track which had brought us up from the village. The cold drizzle petered out as we climbed higher, the sky brightened and when we reached the top of the hill we saw two pillars set back from the road. They were clearly the entrance to a drive now much pitted and covered with vegetation.

'It must be the entrance to Barton Grange.' I said. 'Let's have a look.'

'It's private property,' said Ann. 'We'd be trespassing.'

'No harm in just *looking*' I said.

Ann agreed reluctantly and we began walking along the overgrown drive. After thirty yards it was still winding away in front of us without any sight of the house, and I sensed her unease.

'We've gone far enough,' she said.

'If there's nothing after this next bend, we'll turn back.'

But then a larger, distressed version of our hotel appeared. It was a sad sight with its rust-streaked walls, broken plaster, damp brickwork and rafters jutting jaggedly into the sky.

I wanted to go inside but Ann was adamant.

'I don't know what's in there and nor do you', she said. 'It's creepy and it frightens me.'

'It's only a quick look.'

'Please, please don't do anything stupid,' she said.

Taking that as permission I pushed past the broken front door into the ruined hallway fumbling in the backpack for my torch. The light reassured me in the pitch-black darkness for my footsteps sounded hollow and loud in the silence and I felt intrusive and suddenly vulnerable. At the end of the passage I found a conservatory where large earthenware pots once holding orange trees lay broken and blackened with fungal decay. Panes from the glass ceiling had shattered on the tiled floor and as I gingerly stepped inside the splinters of glass crunched under my weight.

I turned to leave and as I did so I saw a heap of broken wine cases piled up in a corner surrounded by smashed glasses and empty bottles. Judging from the wine labels they had once contained very fine wine. And then in the middle of this wreckage I saw lying there a beautiful, undamaged decanter.

'And what exactly do you propose doing with that?' Ann said, when I rejoined her, holding it carefully.

'It was just abandoned,' I said. 'And it's so lovely.'

'Take it back, it's not ours.'

'If I must,' I said with bad grace, judging it wasn't worth a row but still coveting it. After I'd replaced it, we set off down the hill and reaching our room we both felt cold and chilled.

'I'm going to have a bath,' said Ann and seeing my opportunity I grabbed my rucksack, hurried downstairs, ran up the road and, reaching Barton Grange, I made straight for the conservatory. Only the sound of my breathing and a distant drip of water disturbed the dead silence as I reached the place where I'd seen the decanter. I stretched out my hand and grasped it by the neck but as I lifted it, I thought I heard a sigh. Rattled, I crammed it into my backpack, turned round and tore down the corridor and out into the darkness. I sped along the track into the hotel drive and breathing heavily stuffed the decanter into the boot of the car. When I came back to the room, Ann, who was getting dressed looked closely at me.

'What have you been up to?' she said.

There are few secrets between us because I always look guilty after deceiving her so I told her what I'd done.

'You *fool!*' she said. 'Be it on your own head and conscience.'

I felt guilty, but guilty pleasure is still pleasure, however fleeting.

★ ★ ★

When we came down for our pre-dinner drink, we found the sitting room shadowy, illuminated only by the firelight and candles, giving it a nice preChristmassy touch. In the gloom an elderly couple were sitting quietly on the sofa facing the fire and as we came into the room the man turned and smiled at us.

'Giles and Edith Sheldon,' he said, politely rising, and I introduced us. It was rather hard to see very clearly in the dim light, but I noticed he was tall and thin, with a neat moustache and dressed in rather outdated clothes which would always look well-made and expensive. Because they were. He was wearing a cravat which I had abandoned long before but only with reluctance for I'd always thought how *complete* they made you look. He spoke with a clipped upper class accent using precise phrases.

'First time here?' he asked, and I nodded.

'We've been coming here for many years,' said Edith.

She looked elegant in her long silken dress and like Giles spoke carefully and clearly. I judged them to be well into their eighties and warmed to them for their style and manners.

'At Christmastide,' she continued. 'We always met at the big house.'

'Seat of a good family,' said Giles, nodding. 'Good stock.'

'Charlie Ames was always a good host,' added Edith.

'Kept a damn fine cellar,' said her husband. 'Did up this place for his mater and with her gone he came here.'

'It didn't change anything,' said Edith. 'Old school rules to the end.'

'Family made a fortune importing wine from Bordeaux,' said Giles. 'Only trade fit for a gentleman. Had relatives trading in Porto and Madeira, too. *Cadet* branch, of course, but respectable enough, I dare say.'

'May I get you a drink?' I asked. 'I'm sure Martina will be here in a moment.'

'Most kind, but sadly we must decline,' said Giles. 'Mustn't *linger* – just like to check if the old place's still in one piece.'

'And is it?'

'Pretty well,' he said. 'Old Charlie will kick up if anything too much is changed as your hostess knows only too well!' He smiled and as he rose I stood up to let his wife pass. *Odd that we hadn't shaken hands*, I thought.

'What a charming couple,' said Ann. 'How pleasant it is to be here tonight with nice people like them.'

Martina then bustled in with two newly arrived guests and I ordered our wine. We made small talk with the brash couple before we were called to our usual table.

'It's rather dim in there,' she said, when we reached the dessert. 'And it's rather late but I'm sure the couple we met *are* there in the conservatory. There's someone with them who seems angry about something, but it's hard to see what's going on.'

'Let me see,' I said, impatient as usual, twisting around in my seat.

'You'll do no such thing,' said Ann. 'And you're not to stare at them. What's got into you tonight?'

She got up and I followed her out of the room for she was right. Since the decanter episode I'd felt anxious and unsettled and back in our room I apologised.

'Let's just move on,' she said. 'It's really cold outside and the room's warmed up at last. Hopefully we'll get a good night's sleep.'

★ ★ ★

It was three o'clock. A terrible nightmare had woken me and sick with horror, I'd slipped into the bathroom to bathe my face. As I dried my hands I glanced out of the window and my heart missed a beat. The moon, appearing from behind scudding clouds was bathing the carpark below in a cold light outlining a bent figure near our car. It was like a hound sniffing around for a fox's scent but somehow more horribly *furtive*. Then the moon went behind a cloud and when it reappeared I saw nothing below.

I was more frightened than I'd ever been in my life before, but I knew that what I had to do would mean somehow overcoming my terrible fears. My hands trembled as I threw on some clothes and Ann stirred in her sleep as I gently opened the door. All was quiet as I stole down the stairs and along the hallway and when I opened the front door the cold night air nearly took my breath away.

I crossed to the carpark, opened the car boot, stuffed the decanter into my rucksack and quietly closed the lid. For a moment when I stood up I felt faintly ridiculous but then fear flooded back like an irresistible tide. My legs felt weak, but I turned and ran up the drive as fast as I could racing along the moonlit drive almost sobbing with fear. Then I was up the hill and through the twin pillars and along the driveway to the Grange talking nonsense to reassure myself. Before the house I took a deep breath and my courage in both hands and stepped into the blackness of the hallway. I found myself shouting *'I'm sorry! I'm sorry!'* as I crunched my way across the conservatory floor.

The beam from my torch flickering in front of me had been only a shade less frightening than the darkness but as I went to take the decanter out of my rucksack, the flashlight fell out of my hand and the night rushed in. Something grabbed at the vessel but sobbing I hung on to it until the pressure eased and it was still intact when I laid it gently where I'd found it. Then I turned and raced blindly along the passage out into the drive and down the hill for dear life.

Reaching the hotel grounds, I'd half expected to find the place a blaze of lights and all hell let loose, but everything seemed quite normal. That brought me back to my senses and shivering with cold I crept up the stairs and into our room. Ann was fast asleep as I took off my outdoor clothes and got into bed, exhausted but profoundly relieved. And I slept like the dead until she woke me at eight o'clock.

★ ★ ★

'I hope you enjoyed your stay,' said Sarah to Ann, as we were checking out, the next morning.

'Very much,' said my wife. 'Please thank everyone for us.'

'Of course,' she said, smiling faintly.

Ann said goodbye and went out to the car carrying her small suitcase.

'Anything I can help you with?' said Sarah looking hard at me after rearranging the papers on her desk.

'In the sitting room last night we met a charming couple,' I said. 'My wife thought she saw them later in your conservatory. Would you please give them our best wishes and season's greetings when you see them?'

'It's highly unusual for guests to meet them,' she said, coldly. 'What did they say to you?'

'They remembered coming here at this time of the year and spoke of Lord Ames liking to find things as he remembered them,' I said. 'And the gentleman said you knew that.'

'It would have been less distressing all round if you'd heeded those words before you did what you did,' she said. 'When he got back his Lordship was playing merry hell with all of us. Thank goodness you put it back.'

'You *knew* about the decanter?' I stammered.

'Word gets around,' she said, with an icy smile.

'But how?'

'Because they saw you take it.'

'But there was no one there.'

'Not a living soul,' she said. 'But you disturbed those who *were* there, and they didn't take kindly to that. Now here's your bill and I trust you enjoyed your stay. And don't worry, I'll see your good wishes are passed on to Lord and Lady Sheldon.'

'But... but...' I muttered.

'Just *accept* some things,' she said. 'It's clear they liked you, and perhaps you'll return this time next year.'

'Thank you,' I said, hurriedly taking the bill and picking up the suitcases.

'Goodbye,' she said. 'Or should I say *au revoir!*'

'I think we'd better say "Goodbye" for now' I said, picking up our suitcases.

'Well, if you change your mind, I know the Sheldon's would be delighted to see you,' she said.

And do you know we've been back with them every Christmas after our terrible traffic accident going home. We always love every minute of being with them and wouldn't miss our annual visit for the world!

WORDS

I could always plough a straight furrow and help cows calving but "words" were always too slippery for me to get a handle on. I could break in any old bronco with a rope for a rein, but lassoing letters was just not my thing.

I was the eldest and when Pa died, I had the farm. Ma had passed some time before and with all my brothers gone I got lonesome. It was then it came to me that I needed a wife. Other men had wives, even Pa had managed it, and he was the meanest critter you could hope not to meet. And musing over it one night on the seat on the porch I figured out that to get one worth having I'd need *words*. But when I met a girl, especially one I liked, they just wouldn't come.

So I figured I could get someone to do it for me – a "spokesman" so to speak, just like hiring a vet or a cowhand. Tell him what I wanted to say and then I'd do the rest. Now I only had two problems between me and my bride: I didn't have a girl and I didn't have a talker.

Then I met Janine at a barn dance, and I had a mind to wed her. That only left one problem. So I went to the city to find me a talker and met a real smooth city gent called Eddie in a bar. He told me he was a professional storyteller and was offering me a special deal on account of the great drought affecting his business. He'd done all manner of things in life and recounted his exploits so well I felt they'd happened to me. And that was with only a few of my drinks inside him!

He told me that his two brothers in life were fantasy and enchantment, And I signed him up on the spot as he seemed a real good bet to impress a girl. We arranged that he'd come to help me out when the occasion was right and we left it there. But before I left town I hung around a bit and met this other man who'd known him. He told me Eddie was a seed salesman down on his luck who'd lived in a kind of fantasy world after his wife died. And as for enchantment I found out the hard way he could sure spin a girl a good yarn. Because after they'd met, Janine and seedy ran off together with 20 dollars of my hard-earned money.

So I wrote myself a note saying I was giving up on words and investing my money in the offensive weaponry department in case I rubbed up against Eddie or anyone else talking too fancy!

★ ★ ★

That's where my story really ended – or so I thought.

It turned out that Janine's little sister Dolly heard about what had happened and came by one day with some fruit from their orchard and a few kind words to say how sorry she was. Seemed she'd seen me at the barn dance and hoped we'd have a dance but we never did. Funny really. I felt I could talk quite well with her.

Anyway, sometime later Janine and her seed salesman met Elmer, who crowed like a full blown cockerel, making Eddie sound like a poor wet hen. Next thing she's off with Elmer and when he dumps her she then high-tails it home, expecting the great welcome from me.

I was on the porch whittling a stick when she arrived, dolled up like she's going to a dance or something.

'Hello Charlie,' she says. 'I've decided to come back to you.'

Just then Dolly comes out of the kitchen where she's been baking and stares at her sister as if she'd returned from the dead.

'What are you saying to my Charlie?' she says.

'*Your* Charlie,' says Janine, going a bit red about the gills. '*Your* Charlie!'

'And what are you doing on my porch?' says Dolly, wiping her hands on her apron.

'*Your* porch,' says Janine. 'Since when, I'd like to know!'

'Since we was wed,' said my wife.

Heavens above, talk about a torrent of words cascading out of those two and just *flying* through the air that still night, so fast and furious it fair made my head spin! I couldn't grasp *everything* of what was said, but I got the sense.

And that's made me think it's not such a bad thing to just get on quietly with the ploughing and let Dolly sing away in her kitchen! You don't always need a lot of words to tell others how much you care for them. There are other ways of doing that.

THE GREAT TEDDY BEAR ROBBERY

'The lowest and vilest alleys in London do not present a more dreadful record of sin than the smiling and beautiful countryside,' Sherlock Holmes once remarked to Dr Watson, and Inspector Clench of the Hampshire Constabulary would be the first to agree with him. And that was why he had his eye on both the Millhouse on the River Trimble and Wayne Greasley.

The river was a world-renowned chalk stream, most of whose fishing rights were privately owned and whose natural unpolluted state promoted the fame of its native trout as well as accounting for their high mortality rate. Pretty thatched cottages lined the river and in the picturesque village of Much Trimble they commanded huge prices. Lured by greed many locals had long ago sold up and moved away but some of their offspring still lived in a shabby estate in the village. Many of them were unemployed having learned nothing at the former local school where their attendance was as useless to them as it was intolerable for the staff.

Wayne, once one of these pupils and the bane of Clench's life was now living with his sister Sherene who spent her days in a dressing gown watching reality television while her ex-con partner, Jez, peddled dirty drugs in the nearby town. Wayne, when he could stir himself did a bit of burglary, somehow managing to avoid detection, but robbing frightened old folk of their pensions, although easy money, didn't generate enough income and recently he'd been thinking about raising his game. And that was where the Millhouse as the most desirable property on the Trimble came in.

Since the early Middle Ages there'd been a structure on the site using water diverted from the main stream to power the water wheel and after it ceased working it passed through a succession of private hands. Much gentrified, it emerged from the nineteenth century as an elegant Georgian house with well-kept lawns and river frontage. It was currently owned by Carl Zollweger, a Swiss financier who bought it as part of a larger estate, but it was seldom used by his family who preferred Paris, London and New York. Consequently, it was often let out to consortia like wealthy Japanese anglers wanting to practice their *tenkara* skills on the river and the local cleaners and gardeners who worked for them and other rich tenants spoke in awe of their costly possessions.

Rural policing relies heavily on local contacts, and among the Inspector's allies was Giles Price, a local auctioneer and estate agent. Respected enough to handle the letting of the Millhouse he also helped the police when dubious goods turned up for auction. In return he enjoyed generous parking rights in the village and inside information on a number of potential housing sales. Wayne had his contacts too, for many of the pretty cottages and period houses relied on local labour to clean and service them and when he heard that removal people had turned up at the property he sensed an opportunity. And that explained the inspector's concern, for any trouble at the Millhouse would attract the attention of his superiors, and in any case he had a score or two to settle with young Greasley.

Now things were moving quickly and Wayne hurried down to the river to see what was going on. The contents of the furniture vans intrigued him as expensive suitcases were followed by exotic furniture like gold embellished side tables, low beds, strangely shaped sofas, embroidered cushions and brightly patterned fabrics and curtains. None of this would have come as a surprise to Inspector Clench for Giles had informed him that two Middle Eastern families had taken the place for a year and that meant resident wives, numerous children and professional security guards.

Meanwhile, to Wayne's astonishment, the next possessions to be unloaded included a tall, black wardrobe covered in silver stars, a selection of golden cages, something like an upended fish tank and what looked like a huge darts board surrounded by light bulbs. These were followed by expensive dolls, balloons and costumes with sparkling sequins on long clothes racks followed by a collection of Teddy Bears. Wayne stared, for in the middle of the ursine collection was the largest teddy bear he'd ever seen standing at least five feet high. But as it was being carried into the house a large, black Mercedes swept into the drive behind the vans and his heart sank for inside were four well dressed men, obviously armed professional security guards. Right out of his league.

At last the removal men drove away and after satisfying themselves that all was secure the guards also left, locking the front door behind them. As yet Wayne could see no sign of the new occupants or Inspector Clench who'd planned to be there for the removals but had been delayed by traffic. He was aware that he must act quickly and knew what he had to do, for the most unsavoury part of his shabby life was delivering graphic child pornography to Edgar Slymer, a local family solicitor. Wayne acted as middleman for Jez who obtained the hard copy images for the lawyer who was too cunning to go online.

'Just an innocent hobby,' Slymer confided in Wayne. 'Wouldn't touch a kiddie, or anything like that. I just like children and what's the harm in seeing a few innocent pictures of them?

And anything in the *toy* line you might come across let me know, but mum's the word.' Wayne hadn't enquired into the use to which such toys might be put but remembered the conversation and saw an opportunity.

He wandered over to the house and, after looking around to make sure he was unobserved, glanced in through the front window and seeing no sign of anyone inside he ran round to the rear of the building. Skilled at breaking and entering he forced open a window, climbed into the kitchen and opened the back door from inside. He then looked around.

Spotting the huge bear on a gold-patterned low sofa he quickly stuffed it into a large black, plastic sack he'd seen in the kitchen. Dragging it through the house and out of the back door he hefted it onto his back and set off for Slymer's house where he expected a warm welcome followed by a rapid exchange of currency. But he was the last person the lawyer wanted to meet, especially after a bad day in court.

'What the hell do you want?' he said. 'I've told you not to come round here unless we agreed to meet.'

'Got you a bear, Mr Slymer,' said Wayne, pointing to the heavy bulging sack he'd brought.

The solicitor snorted but looked in the sack.

'You bloody fool, Greasley,' he said. 'What the hell do I want with that? Just bugger off and take that thing with you.'

'You've no cause to take on like that, Mr Slymer,' said Wayne defiantly. 'You forget what I knows 'bout you.'

'Yes, and I knows a lot more 'bout you,' hissed the lawyer. 'So fuck off, you scum if you don't want to get into real trouble.'

Wayne sullenly humped the great bundle onto his back and went home to his sister's place, where he dumped it in the skip in the yard next door. Then he went into the empty house, took a six-pack of lager out of the fridge to drink as a chaser and a quart bottle of cider he'd lifted from the Co-op and spent the evening watching football on the television.

★ ★ ★

When Inspector Clench arrived late at the Millhouse he was in a very bad mood. Finding the front door open he walked into the dim hallway where he found a pale, tall silver-haired man wearing a long grey coat standing and musing as he inspected the items the removal men had delivered. He turned with a start when the Inspector approached him.

'And you are, Sir?' said Clench, after introducing himself, and showing his identity card.

'Thomas Revett,' said the man, with a slight bow. 'In theatrical circles known as the "Great Mephisto". You are perhaps familiar with the name?'

'Sadly not, Sir,' said Clench slowly, playing the old plod ploy. 'My knowledge of the acting profession is not what it should be.'

'From time to time, Inspector,' said the man, with a theatrical gesture, 'I'm *engaged* to use my modest talents to help children settle into their new surroundings.'

'Staying here are you, Sir?' said Clench.

'I forget... 'Randells?'' said the man absently, continuing his study of the furniture.

'A very nice hotel, I'm given to believe,' said Clench, aware of its astronomical rates.

'No doubt,' was the reply. Then, after a pause, Revett said. 'There's been a break-in through the back window in the kitchen, Inspector.'

They both inspected the damage and the open back door.

'Anything of value taken?' Clench asked, recognising Greasley's signature on the break-in.

'Only a bear.'

'And what kind of bear would that be, Sir?'

'A very large one, commonly referred to as a "Teddy Bear".'

'Distinguishing marks?'

52

'Such bears look alike, Inspector,' said Revett. 'But this is very special.'

'Because of its size, Sir?'

'Partly, but its uniqueness lies in its *nature,*' he said. 'Never fear, Inspector, it will find its way back to me and the thief will be punished. You smile? You disbelieve my assertion?'

'Nothing would give me greater pleasure than your words coming true, Sir,' said Clench. 'But sadly, I must rely on more traditional police methods of detection.'

'Happily, I am not limited by such constraints,' laughed Revett. 'Soon, I will have my bear, and if you wish, you will have your man.'

If only, thought the Inspector. *If only.*

★ ★ ★

When Wayne awoke the next morning, he was lying on the dirty settee in his sister's living room fully dressed and feeling terrible. He fumbled for a cigarette and cursed when he remembered he'd finished his last package the night before. Dizzy and nauseous he staggered across the room to see what he could find in the kitchen and fell over an enormous teddy bear.

He gazed blearily at the creature before kicking it out of his way and finding nothing he wanted in the kitchen came back and sat on the settee. He scratched his head trying to piece together last night's events and regarded the huge bear which returned his unsteady gaze with unwinking, brown eyes. Recalling with distaste his meeting with Slymer, he was sure he'd come back afterwards with the bear and dumped it in the skip next door. But he'd only stolen *one* bear so what was it doing here? Maybe Sherene had seen it in the skip and brought it in. Yes, that was it. But why would she do that? He could hear her moving about upstairs and shouted up to her.

'Wot is it? And wot you doin' last night?' she said, coming down the stairs, looking at him and then the bear. 'Wot you want with a great thing like that?'

'Why did you take it out of the skip, you silly cow, you?' said Wayne.

'You still pissed?' she said. 'Why would I do that?'

'Don't you want it, then?'

'No, I bleedin' don't and get it out of the house before Jez gets down,' she said, looking fearfully upstairs.

'Alright, alright,' he mumbled. 'I'm going, I'm going.' He kicked the bear along the floor and then hoisted it up and lugged it to the yard next door where he heaved it back into the empty skip.

When he came back his sister, who'd been using the bathroom while he'd been gone and had lit a cigarette, nodded at the bear on the settee.

'I thought you was goin' to get rid of the bloody thing,' she said.

'I just put it in the skip,' Wayne said.

'You can't have, can you?'

'But I told you I fuckin' did,' he shouted.

'Well obviously you fuckin' din't,' she shouted back.

'Wot's goin' on?' said a deep voice, and Jez's large shape came to the top of the stairs. He looked down and shouted, 'Can't get no sleep with your bloody racket goin' on. And wot's that bleedin' thing doing down there?'

Wayne gave a cry, sat down with his head in his hands, feeling so awful he wished he could die, a sentiment shared by his sister's partner.

'Wot's up with 'im?' said Jez, looking Eric, and then Sherene.

'Dunno, he turned up with the bear last night,' she said. 'Dunno where he got it.'

'Bloody well tell 'im to get rid of it.'

''Es tryin' to, Jez, honest,' she said. 'But it keeps comin' back.'

'That's just crap,' shouted Jez. 'I'm goin' back to bed and if there's a fuckin' bear when I come down, Sher, your baby brother's goin' get a real hiding. Savvy, Wayne!'

'Wayne, take it back, luv,' said Sherene. 'He means what he says.'

★ ★ ★

Inspector Clench spent the next three days in his office in the local town and when he returned to the village, he found a pile of paperwork on his desk. He was about to start when the local resident officer, Sergeant Oates knocked on the door,

'Someone outside to see you, Inspector,' he said. 'Came round late last night. I told him you'd be back, today.'

'It's only eight o'clock, Sarge,' said Clench. 'Can't it wait?'

'He's in a bad way,' said Oates. 'Best see him, Sir.'

'Who is it?'

'Young Wayne Greasley. Poor kid.'

'Oh, get him in, Sarge.'

Wayne looked truly awful after two nights sleeping rough. His face was horribly bruised and misshapen with dirty sticking plaster covering the cuts and abrasions. There was also a bandage on his right arm heavily soaked in blood.

'You need medical treatment,' said Clench. 'Why didn't you go to the Accident and Emergency Unit at the hospital?'

'No way,' said Wayne. 'But I wan' police protection.'

'Who from?' said Clench, who knew all about Jez's vicious temper.

'From this bear.'

'That your idea of a joke, son?' said the inspector. 'If it is I'll have you for wasting police time, insulting behaviour and much else that will come to my fertile mind.'

'No, no, Mr Clench, Sir,' said Wayne, suddenly a teenager found scrumping apples. 'Jez roughed me up alright, but I deserved it. It was the bear what done it. Got us all down – me an Sher and 'im. It wouldn't go away Mr Clench, it wouldn't go away. It won't ever go away.'

'Steady, lad,' said Clench, for Wayne, weeping with distress had grabbed his arms for support.

'I take it out and dump it,' cried Wayne. 'But it comes back. And it's clever, Mr Clench, it's *clever.* It waits until no one can see it appear. But it always does! It always comes back!'

'Look lad, you've had a bad time and by the look of your arm, you've lost a lot of blood,' said the inspector. 'Still handy with the knife Jez, I see. You'll feel calmer when we've got that looked at.'

'Why did you lift the bear in the first place, Wayne?' he said gently. He didn't know about reappearing bears, but he knew a lot about getting at the truth if you went about it in the right way.

'I done it for Mr Slymer,' cried Eric. 'But he din't want it, and he threw me out.'

'Mr Slymer?' said Clench. 'You mean the *solicitor?*'

And then it all came out. Jez, Slymer and every other robbery that Wayne had carried out. That was a lot of information, but Clench kept the paperwork to a minimum and a tearful Wayne signed the lot.

'Now I'm going to get Sergeant Oates to go with you to the hospital for medical treatment,' said the inspector.

'No charges against Jez, please, Mr Clench, Sir,' pleaded Wayne. 'He'll kill me, else.'

'Domestic abuse affair, I'm not interested,' said the inspector. 'But I fancy Mr Jez will be answering some other questions, believe me.'

'What about the bear? The bear?'

'I'll go and see the owner,' said the Inspector. 'Don't you worry, lad, we'll sort this out.'

★ ★ ★

After they'd gone the inspector walked over to the Millhouse and knocked on the front door. It was opened by a youngish man whose cheerful face was lined with laughter lines.

Clench introduced himself, and the man smiled and offered his hand.

'I don't know if I can help, Inspector,' he said. 'I'm only here for a week or two. I'm the entertainer for the kids – Peter Welles is my name but you might know me as Mr Tomato!'

'It was your colleague I really wanted to speak to, Mr Tomato – Mr Welles, I should say,' said Clench.

'Colleague, Inspector?' smiled the man. 'You must be mistaken There's only me here. Even the children haven't arrived yet.'

'It was Mr Revett, who you may know as "The Great Mephisto".'

'You must be joking, Inspector,' said Welles, laughing. 'It couldn't be Jack *Revett*! I saw him when I was very young. What a magic touch he had with youngsters and how they loved him. He was known as "The Children's Friend," but he died years ago.'

'I spoke to him here,' said Clench. 'He said he was staying at Randalls.'

'Wish I was,' laughed Welles.

'Excuse me for a moment,' said the inspector. He went into the sitting room and used his mobile to ring the hotel who confirmed that no guest called Revett had recently stayed there.

He returned to Welles and asked if all his equipment was in order.

'Odd you should say that,' he replied. 'Everything's here, but I seem to have inherited a giant bear.'

'How strange,' said Clench, one step ahead of a professional magician for the first time in his life.

★ ★ ★

The "Great Child Pornography Scandal", first exposed by Inspector Clench ("Clench of the Schoolyard") was the turning point in his career. Wayne and Jez turned out to be the tiny tip of a very nasty business that kept Interpol detectives busy for months. But the outcome was worth every second of time and all the money put into it for its success protected a whole generation of children.

After his promotion, Superintendent Clench left the village for greater things but occasionally drove past the Millhouse when going about his business. Unfailingly modest about his detective work he'd long since stopped feeling guilty about an encounter with a deceased magician which led to the safeguarding of so many young ones. Who would have believed him, anyway? For after he'd made some discreet inquiries none of the furniture delivery men or security guards remembered seeing the Great Mephisto.

He was content to bask in the warm feelings he felt towards a man he'd never known in life, greatly loved by the little ones and indeed a true "Children's Friend". And to judge from his performance in Much Trimble, he was as effective in real life as he was as a stage magician. In spite, of course, of also being dead at the same time!

PAYBACK TIME

'Leslie,' said Grace. 'Do you remember the last time you paid for something in the big supermarket?'

'Do you want the date, or will a year do?' said her husband. 'Why are you asking?'

'I was just thinking,' she said. 'With Christmas coming we must put more into the old people's club.'

'Don't worry, they won't go short.'

'Just thought I'd mention it,' she said, getting up to make another pot of tea.

★ ★ ★

It was twelve-thirty, and the kindly old pair were sitting down to their dinner known in more polite circles as "lunch". There was steak and kidney pie with greens on the side, a slice or two of bread and butter and for afters an apple tart with double cream washed down with sugary cups of builders' tea. The pie and over-cooked veg. came *gratis* from a large German supermarket as did the rice pudding, coldly congealing beneath its dark, shiny skin. And the tea, after maturing for some time in an old brown teapot, a shade tepid with bitter tannic overtones, was fresh lifted that morning from Tesco's and going down a treat. Good traditional English fare and they were tucking in with relish.

Grace's comment was not a rebuke to Leslie's habitual criminality– a proclivity they shared, but simply a reminder that Christmas was nearly upon them. Lifelong socialists of the old school, they didn't see their illegal activities as wrong or themselves as villains, but rather righters of social wrongs. They never took from a corner shop or the Co-op but were more than happy to "redistribute" the proceeds of their retail activities to the needy from the grasping hands of rich capitalists like supermarket-chain owners. They kept a meticulous record of their "purchases," never allocated funds that they couldn't account for and had no political affiliation of any kind.

'Mrs Patel's daughter's going to have her baby very soon,' said Grace, passing Leslie a second helping of rice pudding. 'She's in Leicester, and they'll be away for a few days.'

'Bad luck for his business with Christmas coming up and things not going too well for him,' said her husband. 'Carrot-head will have to do a bit of work in the shop for once.'

'I wish you wouldn't call him that,' said Grace. 'It's quite a nice shade of auburn and Darren does his bit. He carries things to the car for lady customers and if he gets a little tip it's always, "Thank you, madam". And a nice smile too, even if he doesn't really mean it.'

'Oh, he likes the ladies all right, does Carroty,' Leslie said. 'And as for carrying things for customers, carrying on with staff's more like it. That blondie sales-rep. with her special promotions for a start.'

'I wish you wouldn't be so crude,' said Grace, getting up from the kitchen table. 'You're not in the "Ferret and Trousers", now.'

'No,' said Leslie, with a hint of regret in his voice.

'And the washing up won't do itself,' she said. 'And when you've done that take the car down to Mr Patel's and get what's on this list, which I wrote with you reading the paper with your feet up all morning and the coal to bring in.'

Driving to the cheerful, grubby little corner shop owned and run by Mr Patel for forty years, Leslie's mind went back to the oppression the gentle Sikh had faced from locals in the working-class neighbourhood when he took over from surly old Treadmill. Everyone forgot how rude, understocked and overpriced that old bastard had been. But with the new owners came the boycott and the broken windows, the slogans and the hate mail. And the Patel kids, in their neat school uniforms endured long years of being sworn and spat at in the street and the playground. They were successful lawyers now...

Somehow Patel Senior, always polite and helpful, had stuck it out over the years, working all hours, and slowly, slowly things improved until now, in the less tight-knit but still strong local community he was fully accepted. But the dark rings under his eyes and the tremor of his hand betrayed the toll taken by forty years of early morning starts and constant worry.

Darren, his assistant was a raw-boned, streetwise lout who Mr Patel had taken on as a favour to his widowed mother. Helpful and pleasant when it suited him the boy was idle and light-fingered when no one was looking. He didn't fool Leslie for a moment. He'd seen him winking at schoolkids stealing sweets and crisps when Mr Patel's back was turned and rather too frequently carrying boxes from the stock room at the back of the shop to where he kept an old car.

Leslie respected and liked Mr Patel very much and had been feeling increasingly guilty about doing nothing to prevent what was going on, especially now the shop was going through a bad patch.

'I carry all the right lines, there are plenty of customers and I work all the hours, Leslie,' Mr Patel had confided in him. 'But the figures just don't add up. I've been making less and less profit for three years running. How can that be?'

That was about the amount of time that Darren had been working in the shop, Leslie thought, remembering how Mr Patel had given them tick several times to tide them over when he was laid up or Gracie took ill. Leslie didn't forget things like that, and his inaction chafed his conscience like an over-scratched sore.

'Did you remember to get a bottle of wine?' said Grace, not looking up from her sewing when he returned from shopping and began unloading his purchases in the kitchen.

'I've done better than a bottle, Gracie,' he said, holding his back as he straightened up after lugging a heavy cardboard case of wine onto the table. 'Just look at that! A round dozen!'

'You haven't bought all those!' she gasped, staring at the case of wine. 'There's Petit Chablis and Fleurie as well as the Bordeaux Superior. However much did you pay for them?'

'The price is on the labels,' he said, starting to put some vegetables into the fridge. 'And I picked out some of the ones we like.'

Grace found her glasses and peered at the price-tag on the nearest bottle.

'It says £18,' she cried. 'Oh, Leslie what have you done? We can't drink all that over Christmas!'

'Then we can give a few away to folks who don't have anything to drink at all, can't we, old girl?'

'Whatever were you thinking of?'

'I thought I'd seen those wines on special offer in the local supermarket and when I checked it out, they were priced, on average, at only £15 a bottle. And £18 on our bottles was the *old* price before Mr Patel reduced his to £15 to compete with the big boys.'

'What are you getting at?' said Grace.

'I saw that precious young man of yours in the shop, changing the new sale prices on the bottles back to the old ones,' he said, looking critically at the blemishes on some oranges he'd "liberated" on the way home from the supermarket. 'Didn't let him know I'd seen him, of course.'

'But why would he do that, Leslie? Was that wrong?'

'Of course, it was, love. The customer pays the old, higher price that nasty Carrot-head put back on the bottle, he rings up the new lower price for the till and keeps the difference. And you can bet it's not just wine and not just at Christmas he's been doing things like that. He's been bleeding poor old Mr Patel dry for three years with his tricks. Nice little earner the wine though, big mark-up for him what with his Christmas bonus and a few old sillies like us giving him a box as well.'

'But that's awful,' said Grace. 'Didn't you say anything to him?'

'He'd only have denied it,' said Leslie. 'And changed the price tags back before Mr Patel returned. But I didn't let him get away with it.'

'Oh, Leslie what did you do?' Gracie wailed, wringing her hands. 'What have you done?'

'I waited until the shop was empty and then had one of my giddy turns,' said Leslie. 'And your Darren, credit give when credit's due, got me a chair and helped me sit down. I had to hold on to him as he lowered me down – you know how my back takes me.'

'I worry about you, all the time, Leslie,' said Grace tearfully. 'What happened then?'

'The old hands may not be what they were, but I can still pick a pocket and I had the wallet out of his back pocket in a jiffy. I took most what was in it-bulging it was!'

'Oh, Leslie that was *stealing*,' said Grace.

'When he came back with a glass of water I put the wallet, minus the notes back in his pocket,' said Leslie. 'And used his money to pay for the wine at the higher old price. I even got him to help me carry it to the car!'

'You should have told him that what he was doing was wrong. He'll only go on doing it, you know he will.'

'I'm going to drop off an envelope later this afternoon which I expect he'll think is his Christmas box,' said Leslie. 'In it there'll be a note saying I knew what he's been up to and that I "used" his own money to pay for the wine, at the old price. And what's left over will make a "contribution" to the "Children in Crisis" appeal.'

'That's nice,' said Grace, approvingly. 'How awful he's been, and at this time of year, too!' But I'm still going round to his mum's and taking one of these bottles because she gets lonely and very down about this time of year.'

'And I'll say that if he doesn't mend his ways plus a hefty gift to celebrate the birth of the Patels' new grandchild,' continued Leslie, 'I'll put the word around. And I can guarantee that a few local lads I know from the gym with the karate club will be coming his way with a view to helping him see things a bit more clearly.'

'If you think it will help dear.'

'And maybe, just *maybe* if he behaves himself next year, we'll ask him and his mum round for our famous, silver service festive "Burnt Turkey and Burgundy Banquet".'

'With the best Worchester dinner set, solid silver candlesticks and decent wine glasses, too', said Grace.

'And when the Patels come back we'll be able to give them a proper season's greeting,' Leslie laughed. 'Knowing it's going to be a more prosperous New Year for them all. I'll make sure of that you can depend on it!'

'Darren will come round in time, Leslie,' Grace said. 'When you were his age you were just the same, and just look at how you've changed! Honest as the day is long!'

THE LAST WORD

D oris was polishing the china dogs on the mantelpiece and
  Charlie had very nearly finished his elaborate scale model
  of St Pancras Station using matchsticks. Nine months in
the making and the end in sight at last! Just a few more touches
to the façade and it would be done. He began to edge the last few
matches into place holding his breath with his heart in his mouth.

At that moment a thin parcel squeezed through the front
door letter box by the postman landed with a thump on the
floor and Cindy, their corgi, hated by Charlie almost as much
as she was doted on by Doris, rushed to tear the packing to bits.
Charlie, turning round to shout at the animal, caught his chair
under one of the legs of the trestle table supporting his great
model and down came the table and the Victorian Gothic Grand
Hotel entrance followed by the tower it supported. And after a
little hesitation a large chunk of the south face followed suit and
plunged down in a shower of matches. Hitler's bombers hadn't
even come close to such a destruction of the original building and
Charlie stared numb with shock followed by fury and outrage
at the damage. Doris, now a little deaf, continued her tuneless
humming as she worked and heard nothing.

'Charlie, what I'm going to say is important,' she said to the
wall. 'So do listen, for once.'

'I am listening.'

'I wish you would, just for once.'

'I'm in the middle of a disaster!' he replied, almost in tears.

'You're always in the middle of something when I want to say something to you,' she said, tutting at the dust on the mantlepiece.

'And you're always interrupting,' he said, very quietly.

'What was that?'

'I said I was listening. I *am* listening. I'm all ears. What do you want?'

'Now I've forgotten what I was going to say.'

'That stupid dog of yours has just destroyed nine months of work,' wailed Charlie. 'Nine *months*!'

'Oh, yes I remember,' said Doris. 'Listen out for the doorbell.'

'Wasted! Why do I bother?''

'What did I say?'

'Listen out for the doorbell,' said Charlie. 'Can't promise to hear it. I miss it sometimes.'

'Charlie, you *always* miss it when you don't wear your hearing aid. Why are you getting up?'

'To find my hearing aid, I don't know where I put it.'

'Why don't you wear it all the time?'

'Because it hurts. And you don't wear yours all the time but you need to. And your glasses, too.'

'Now listen, I'm going out to the shops.'

'Where are you going?'

'Does it matter?'

'Not really, unless you're going to pick up two million matches.'

'Oh no, it wouldn't matter to you unless it's something to do with your blessed station,' said Doris. 'Now see what a mess you've made – someone's got to clear that up, and we both know who that'll be.'

'I've saved you some time – it's only half a station now,' said Charlie. 'How long will you be gone?'

'I told you, a few minutes.'

'No, you didn't. And even if you did it would mean anytime, *except* a few minutes.'

'I haven't time for this. Just answer the doorbell if it rings, will you?'

'I might have the telly on to hear the warm-up for the big match!'

'We talked about this yesterday,' said Doris. 'Can't you record it?'

'What good would that do?' said Charlie starting to shove matches into a linen bag. 'I want to watch it *live* from Berlin.'

'I don't care if it's from the moon – I'm going now,' said Doris, going into the cupboard under the stairs to get her coat. 'And Charlie, why do you think you're wearing your Sunday suit?'

'You told me to,' said Charlie, looking at the stain on his trousers she hadn't yet spotted. 'And... remind me...'

'Because a *photographer* is coming from the local paper and we're going to have our *picture* taken.'

'I remember now.'

'And why are we going to have our picture taken?'

'Because... remind me.'

'Because we've been married sixty years, like the other couples in the paper. And what did we agree we'd tell them when the journalist asks us what makes a marriage like ours work?'

'Umm...'

'It's because we've listened to each other and agree on the big things in life.' said Doris, looking into the hall mirror and adjusting her hat. 'That's what I'm telling them, and you said you'd think about adding something else. Have you?'

'Having a shed at the bottom of the garden.'

'I'm going out now. Don't let me find they've missed calling because you were watching football,' said Doris, briskly. 'And don't get anything on your suit if you go on doing that. And remember to make sure your... zip's done up. Not like at Clara's wedding.'

'Is that all?'

'And don't forget to spend a penny before you need to so you don't waste everyone's time when they get here!'

'How can I go before I need to?' said Charlie. 'And what if I'm spending a penny when they ring the doorbell?'

'And don't wiggle your false teeth when you meet the paper people,' said Doris. 'Why you haven't been to see that new dentist, I don't know.'

'Are you going or not?'

'I should have gone years ago.'

'Glad you didn't dear,' said Charlie, checking his flies. 'Or I'd have missed out on the best thing that ever happened to me. I really mean that.'

'Yes, well that's as maybe,' said Doris, checking if she'd got the front door key. 'Off now, dear, back soon. And don't *grimace* when they take the picture. You've got such a nice smile when you want to use it. Charmed me that did, the very first time I saw it – made my knees go weak. And still does, you silly old man, still does.'

GREEN QUEEN'S FINAL SCENE

T he world of plants was always a closed book to me and I'd no wish to change my reading habits after harsh words with a former friend concerning the death of her bonsai in my keeping. And, in spite of feeling it's probably better to fondle than fell them, I've never hugged a tree. As for animals, in Surrey where I grew up mountain gorillas were so rare that having to share a seat with a 400-pound Silverback *en route* to Victoria was very unlikely.

On the other hand, plant-wise, my wife Cynthia tended towards the obsessive, and practically that meant a constant procession of new specimens entering our home nodding briefly to the dying and dead they were replacing. After the misery of a crowded garden centre these plants, looking forward to a calm sanctuary, must have felt an icy chill in arriving at the green equivalent of a field hospital in the Crimea War.

Given this background my shock at learning something really bizarre about my relationship with plants will not surprise you. It happened at the Annual Plant and Flower Fair near Kingston market which Cynthia insisted we attend. And the source of this insight, my entry level into the spiritual world of plants, was

"Madame Meg," who offered ethereal plant guidance to the needy in a canvas gazebo. We'd just arrived at the fair and I was feeling mournful because I dislike carrying pots of little shoots poking their hopeful heads out of the dark soil discovering with short-lived delight a brave new world of sunlight and photosynthesis.

'Stop looking so *morose,* Tom,' said Cynthia. 'Can't you *do* something for half-an hour? You're getting under my feet, and on my nerves.'

'*Where should I go?*' I wondered looking around, innocent of any intended harm to such widely separated organs.

'Why not go over and talk to her?' she said, pointing at the tent where Meg's offerings were prominently displayed.

'What should I ask her?' I said, doubtfully.

'Does it matter?' she said. 'The name of the next winner of the Grand National… I don't know.'

I joined the small queue outside Meg's pavilion which looked as if it had served a sentence or two at a few Glasto festivals. A hoody in front of me, an assortment of ironmongery clinging to his pasty features, squinted at me.

'She got weed in there, Dad?' he said, pointing at the gazebo.

'At those prices?' I said, looking at the list of charges on her grubby 'A' board.

'Why she called "Meg" then?' he said, angrily. 'Fuckin' disgrace, man.'

I shrugged and he turned away, muttering, 'Fuckin' trade description pigs should get onto her.'

That only left in front of me a large, expensively dressed woman with a tiny Yorkshire "teacup" terrier on a pink lead. In addition to its place of origin, its breed and the tartan bow tie around its neck, the guiltless animal incensed me further by defecating delicately in front of the tent entrance.

The woman glanced down and then ignored the deposit.

'You're going to leave that there, are you?' I said to her, at which she gave me a withering look, gathered up the innocent creature, snorted and left. I was now but a tiny turd and a step away from Madame Meg herself.

When she called out "Next", I pushed open the canvas flap and passed through into the yellow light of her musty sanctum. The savant was a bulky, middle-aged woman with a gypsy headcloth perched on an abundant head of unkempt, grey hair sitting behind a flimsy folding table covered with a plastic cloth decorated with spirals and stars. She was wearing an ancient, crumpled Laura Ashley dress two sizes too big for her which I assumed was to enhance her aura of mystical power and disguise her generous curves. Her hands, unlike her hair, had received the full henna treatment with patterns on them like those of a Muslim bride and her fingers, nicotine stained and terminating in chipped, green nail polish, displayed a selection of cheap, gaudy rings.

After grasping my outstretched hand with surprising vigour, she indicated an off-white plastic chair in front of her table upon which I perched, whilst introducing myself.

'I take it that it is a plant-related matter with which you seek guidance, Mr Jode,' she said, grasping my hand and twisting it round like a corkscrew. She then began scowling at my palm, breathing hoarsely.

'Not really,' I said, at last managing to free my hand from the iron grip.

'Are you fond of plants?'

'Some,' I said, cautiously.

'Did you know you were a 'plant sensitive,'' she said.

'Really?' I said, with genuine surprise.

'I do not joke, Mr Hode,' she said, severely. 'And I also perceive that you are a "plant whisperer". That's very rare, indeed.'

'Are you sure?' I said, 'I don't recall *whispering* to any plants, or even knowing one well enough to pass on any green gossip worth the effort. '

'Mr Gode,' she said, sternly. 'Do not permit levity to divert your destiny.'

'I promise I won't.'

'That'll be two pounds for the diagnosis, hand massage and stress release,' she said, sensing our dialogue was becoming unproductive.

'Did I ask for all that?'

'It's what you got,' she said. 'I released a lot of pent up green energy, through my bodily contact with you. You were very blocked – I'm quite exhausted.'

'I don't feel unblocked.'

'Two pounds and fifty pence, to be more precise,' she said. 'Perhaps Mrs Frobisher, the lady over by the returns stall with her son, the Security Advisor, my how he's grown, will help out with any difficulty you have in finding the correct sum.'

I gave her the money which she tucked into the pocket of the jeans beneath the flowing fabric rather diminishing her psychic allure and I made a mental note to appraise the underwear of other Servants of Light I might meet in the future.

'When you go for your meal tonight, Mr Lobe,' said Meg. 'Whisper something to the flower on your table. And when you leave see if it doesn't look better than it did before you addressed it.'

'What should I say to it?'

'Any term of endearment,' she said. 'Imagine it to be your wife.' Little did she know that the person to whom she referred didn't need words of rapture from me while wrestling her way through life's undergrowth.

'I was once fond of a gerbil at school,' I said.

'Very well then,' she said. 'Imagine the plant is a gerbil.'

'But it died on my watch,' I said, tears springing to my eyes. 'I was blamed for that, and my parents fined me my pocket money for six weeks.'

'Mr Robe, we are all stretched at times on the rack of remorse,' she said. 'And speaking of distress I see you are in imminent danger of exceeding the time allocated for your session. All too soon the ticket machine will be clicking up another three pounds.'

'It's gone up a bit, hasn't it?'

'It's now after 2pm, and the generous lunchbreak offer as advertised has now elapsed,' she said,

'Who's going to win the Grand National?'

'If I could tell you that,' she said. 'Do you think I'd be here in a draughty tent talking to you about plants?'

'I'll reflect on your words this evening,' I said with some dignity, and withdrew. I then looked in the racing section of a discarded newspaper on a bench to see who the runners were in the Grand National and chose a name at random so that if Cynthia asked about my session, I could pretend I'd got it from Madame Meg.

★ ★ ★

That evening I looked closely at the table we'd been given and saw on it a vase containing a sagging specimen. It was even money on it being dead or plastic and I asked for another berth.

'*Another* table?' Raj the owner said, looking around the empty room.

'What about that one over there?' I said pointing to one upon which was a tiny vase containing a sickly-looking rose bud.

After we'd sat down and Cynthia had, as usual, complained about the draught, she announced she was going to the ladies.

My big chance, I thought, fixing the wilting bud with a kindly look, noting the black spots and the glistening residue left on its leaves by over-active aphids.

'You sweet little gerbil,' I whispered, and then became aware that Mario, sous chef, waiter, washer-up and all-round idiot was looking at me with a puzzled expression.

'Wine you want, innit,' he said.

'The usual Chilean, please,' I said, and he shuffled off.

'Rose, you look a little run-down,' I whispered and then raising my voice said. 'But you'll soon start putting on weight and be looking green in no time.'

'That's what happened to me when I last had a prawn curry here,' said Cynthia, who'd heard me on her return. 'Have you ordered a full-bodied Barolo to accompany our "Rajah's Royal Feast" or the usual thimbleful of warm Pino Grigio to go with my mutton curry?'

After that I was too preoccupied with ordering, eating and drinking to pay much attention to the rosebud. But when we left, I looked back and as I watched, it came to life, shook its leaves and just *burst* into bloom! I said nothing, because I didn't really believe what I'd seen, and even if I *was* a plant whisperer, I wouldn't know what to do about it.

★ ★ ★

During our meal Cynthia told me our niece Hilary was in England and coming to supper the next day and I was pleased as her daunting intellect reflects so well on my side of the family. She teaches English in America, a bit of an uphill task I'd have thought even at a place like Princeton, but being tenured and published she researches a lot and doesn't have to waste too much time lecturing earnest American co-eds. Sadly though, she shares Cynthia's passion for plants.

And so the next evening, when my wife had gauged enough Chassagne Montrachet had passed my lips to lower my resistance, she said, 'Tom, I want you to listen to what Hilary has to say. She's agreed to address the ladies in my flower arranging circle, and I suggested "Plants in Elizabethan prose, drama and poetry". It'll be a change from "Handy Tips for Busy Hands", and several members are also in a book club.'

'Literati luncheon ladies,' I said, lightheartedly.

'Carry on, Hil,' said Cynthia, with a warning glance at me.

'Uncle Tom, it's a question of getting the right *balance*,' said Hil.

'Not Peter Rabbit and not James Joyce,' I said, pouring out the Chateau Giscours.

'You were a journalist,' said Hil. 'If I read my draft to you, will you tell me what you really think?'

'Darling girl,' I said. 'I'd like to help, but I'm just a semi-retired written out, jobbing hack.'

'Formerly an international prize-winning, newspaper columnist,' said Cynthia. 'And you'll do as Hil asks you.'

'But I don't know much about flowers, even less about poetry, and nothing about the ladies.'

'Before he was the financial editor of a national heavy,' said the wife. 'He'd been a travel correspondent, a cooking expert, a wine buff, a gossip columnist and an agony aunt. He's a professional scribbler who can write anything about nothing. And now he'll listen to your ideas and give his considered opinion.'

And that's exactly what happened. After supper Hil took a deep breath and began.

'Introduction,' she said, which I thought was promising. 'A picture may be worth a thousand words, but a single rose can be worth a library! Women are courted with them, we marry in their midst, make amends with them and are laid to rest together. And writers have used them to great effect.'

Not this one! I thought.

'And then,' said Hil. 'Something "to illustrate Transience". For example Shakespeare says "… women are as roses whose fair flower dies, even when they to perfection grow".'

You're on, Will, I thought. *Are you listening up there?*

'Rich Imagery next,' said Hil. 'Plants have lovely names like "purple milk-vetch" or, "melancholy thistle". And think of the mandrake whose roots were seen as tiny men who screamed when they were uprooted.'

'*I know how they feel,*' I thought with a fixed smile on the face.

'For Victorian ladies flowers carried subtle meanings,' Hil continued. 'Mostly unknown to men.'

'Just the poor saps who had to pay for them,' I said.

'Go on, Hil,' said Cynthia. 'Just ignore him when he says things like that.'

'Local dialects allowed writers to cloak their words in secrecy and invest them with double meanings,' Hil continued. 'Rural England has a treasury of local flower and plant names from which poets have plundered rich rewards.'

'You have such a way with words, Hil!' breathed Cynthia.

I tried not to think of the words a sub-editor on a daily paper with five minutes to their deadline would do to copy like that.

'I hope you're listening, Tom,' said Cynthia.

'Indeed,' I said, brightly.

Then we had Ophelia drowning herself wearing "daisies and long purples," and Cordelia consoling the failing old Lear with rosemary followed by a litany of poisonous and unpleasant plants like deadly nightshade.

Enough, Hil, enough! I thought.

'Turning now to Wordsworth,' said Hil. 'For me the appeal of his daffodils lies in their *untamed quality* giving them a sense of *freedom* which the poet later enjoys at leisure.'

That's quite good, I thought. *But not original, surely?*

'Now suppose the poet came across a ditch full of waste and weeds,' she said. 'Would that give him pleasure? Unlikely. But if, in the middle of this mess there was a single perfect rose. Would that not seem more beautiful than if it was in a bed of similar flowers?'

I agreed, '*Contrast* often works better than mere description,' I said. 'Has anyone ever expressed it better than old Will in the last line of Sonnet 94, when he wrote "Lilies that fester smell far worse than weeds".'

'Well?' she said. 'What do you think?'

'A fine piece of prose,' I said. 'Without doubt the final version will be carefully constructed, beautifully written and full of insight.'

'I know, I know,' said Hil, who's no one's fool. 'So what would you suggest instead?'

'Some time before the talk Cynthia might ask each of her ladies to choose a favourite flower or plant,' I said. 'And then you could relate each plant chosen to a poem or a play, making it more *involving* for your audience. And perhaps a wider selection of verse, from different periods?'

'That's a great idea, Uncle Tom,' said Hil, 'I *knew* mine wasn't going to work!'

'It's far too good to be wasted, Hil darling,' I said. 'Such things never are, we both know that. "There's life in't".'

'And I'll get on to it right away,' said Cynthia. 'And woe betide any lady who doesn't come up with the goods.'

I then told them about Madame Meg and my experience with the plant in the restaurant.

'Cynthia, you might suggest anyone with an ailing plant might bring it along, leave it with us and we'll see if we can help.' I said. 'Just say I'm a plant consultant because I don't really believe the whispering bit – the revived rose was probably a one-off.'

It all worked a treat. The ladies loved being involved and some even left jaded plants with me. I whispered to them words of encouragement, and all of them recovered in time but maybe they would have anyway. And Hil published a book called '*A Potpourri of Poetic Plants,*" which contained well-crafted, accurate descriptions and was enormously popular, while Cynthia was made an Honorary Vice-President of the Flower Arranging Group for life.

★ ★ ★

Word must have got around the plant community about my involvement in Hil's project for our garden plants burgeoned as never before. And then new arrivals began making their way into our green kingdom. Many of these had sturdy, no-nonsense suckers that looked ominous and we called in Henry, an invasive plant specialist. He was sturdy and hairy of limb, with weathered, red-veined cheeks from which grey-flecked mutton-chop whiskers sprouted profusely and had a bluffly cheerful manner – the kind of person you find in life whose calling often involves the transmission of bad news to others.

'A big day for me, Mr Toad,' he said, sucking his teeth. 'Never seen the likes of wot you've got growing here.'

'Wot is it I've got, Henry?' I said, slipping adroitly into the vernacular of weed-world.

'Japanese knotweed, Himalayan balsam and New Zealand pigmy-weed for the main course,' he said, smiling happily. 'With giant hogweed on the side and what looks like cotoneaster surprise and kudzu for afters.'

'Can you get rid of this rich menu?' I asked.

'With great difficulty and some expense, Sir,' he said. 'And no guarantee of permanent erasure.'

'What should I do?'

'Sell up before that knotweed gets going around the house,' he said, sucking his teeth. 'You'll never sell it if you don't.'

I sought out Madame Meg in her gazebo and told her what had happened.

'Don't blame me, Mr Hoad,' she said. 'I merely removed the scales from your eyes.'

'I'd value your advice in dealing with the problem,' I said.

'And you shall have it do not fear,' she said. 'As a member of my Green Advisory Register, the entry fee to which I will waive in your case, you will receive a top quality product much in demand, although a fast-track option is available following a voluntary contribution.'

I paid her fifty pounds on the spot.

'Show me pictures of the problem plants and I will *deter*

them psychically,' she said, but the results were disappointing. I took more photos and showed them to her, but she didn't seem particularly put out.

'They didn't *listen*,' she said. 'They are *thronging* to your garden as their undeniable attraction to you is far greater than their adherence to my strictures.'

'Flattering,' I said. 'But it doesn't solve my problem.'

'Indeed, Mr Woad,' she said. 'Happily, help is at hand, and for a trifling supplement I'll employ more drastic measures.'

'What does that mean?' I said, taking out my wallet.

'It's extreme and I don't like doing it,' she said. 'But I'll visit your garden and put a hex on them.'

'You mean you'll *curse* them.'

'An ugly word and one best avoided,' she said. 'And what I must do I must accomplish alone. Do you possess a *flamethrower*, Mr Deed?'

'No I don't,' I said. 'And I didn't imagine you'd even think of using one.'

'The purifying effect of fire, or "Agni", is a small part of an advanced *ritual*,' she said coldly, and I left it at that.

I still did some freelance correspondence work and shortly afterwards got a commission that took us abroad for two months. I'd left everything to her, and I didn't want to know what she was up to. But whatever it was it seemed to work, for the garden we returned to was orderly and neat although slightly singed in places. And as there were no signs of any further invasion, that was the end of my affair with plants. Or so I thought, until Cynthia reminded me about the next Kingston Fair.

'I'll look in on Madame Meg,' I said when we got there, but when I'd made my way to her gazebo there was a different one in its place. The old couple to whom it belonged knew nothing of her whereabouts and suggested we spoke to the fair organiser.

'Bad business, that,' said the woman. 'Poor soul, strangled in her gazebo, counting her takings after a busy day. A great tragedy, with her always prompt with her rental payments, which is more than I could say about some around here.'

'Murdered?' I said, to keep her on track. 'Any clues as to the perpetrator?'

'Nothing for the police to go on,' she said. 'It was as if something *snaked* into the tent, throttled her and then *slithered* out. All they found were these strange leaves on the ground.'

'What did they look like?'

'I took photos of them,' she said. 'But the police weren't interested and I always meant to ask a specialist to identify them. But somehow… you know how hectic life can be in the plant world!'

'Indeed yes,' I murmured, sadly shaking my head. 'I don't suppose you kept them.'

'As luck would have it, I did,' she said and showed me pictures of some large, heart shaped leaves. She mailed me a copy of one and I sent it over to Hilary, now the official family botanist, without an explanation as to its source.

'I've shown the pictures to my colleagues in the botany department,' she replied after a while. 'And they're extremely puzzled. The leaves seem to be a cross between an extremely fast-growing Kudzu (pueraria montana) and a strangler vine. It's possibly an unknown species and definitely not British. Rather odd to find it in England we all thought.'

'Perhaps not as strange as you think,' I said, thanking her.

★ ★ ★

"I cannot see what flowers are at my feet," Keats wrote in his "Ode to a Nightingale" and Madame Meg no doubt posed that question to whatever was climbing up her leg, before getting a more robust response to her query than the poet did to his. And not one she wanted, not one little bit. Nor would she have relished the publicity her death inspired for when the press found her nickname in the plant world was "Green Queen Mother", sub-editors had a ball and came out with "Green Queen's Crime Scene".

You can think what you like about plants but as for me I'm keeping my head well down. You won't catch me in places like the Palm or Temperate House in Kew Gardens, and you can keep your 'nature trails' and municipal gardens. Give me a concrete car park any day.

Don't even think of being a vegetarian if you know what's good for your health. because that's plain *suicide.* Better stick to meat. And if the Green Mafia find you've been using systemic weed killer, possess a wood burning stove or have grubbed up an orchard I wouldn't want to be in your shoes. Nor do I think you're safe if you've ever used a flame-thrower or have a garden incinerator in the shed.

And be on your guard – always remember why an informer is called a "grass" because it *whispers* so well. And think of potatoes with eyes and stalks of wheat with ears. Believe me they all have race memories like elephants. And don't think when you've come back from the garden centre that plants see as concentration camps with that friendly mulch and fertiliser that that will save you, either.

Think instead of those pretty flowers just *longing* to be riding with you on your last journey in the hearse or on top of your coffin or by the graveside after that tree unexpectedly fell on your car! Or when you slipped on that sticky green patch at the top of those steps which landed you in intensive care. Keep your eyes open and watch where you're going, don't walk on the grass and don't pick the flowers! Don't ever let shrubs catch you listening to "*Gardeners' Question Time*" or even *think* about getting onto the committee of your local gardening club.

Now that I'm back at home the plants have returned bigger and fiercer than ever. I tried whispering to them and then shouting:

'I can't return your passion for me! Go away, go away!' but it was no good. And then I did the stupidest thing I've ever done in my entire life – I threatened them with a flamethrower. It was as if the sun had gone behind the clouds in the garden and all the warmth and love shrivelled and died. And the next day not a trace of them remained.

But hell hath no fury like a Kudzu scorned and one day, probably quite soon, I know exactly what's going to happen. Their big enforcer and hit plant, the deadly *Pueraria Montana,* will be paying me a visit, and I'll be joining Meg in her tent in the sky telling me what I did wrong and offering me an unrepeatable opportunity!

And I'll tell her that if she hadn't started using a damned flamethrower in our garden in the first place, we'd all still be together: Cynth and me and dear old Hil, with an improving poem and all of us drinking a bottle of decent wine and an award-winning garden in which to enjoy it. Some hopes now, and all thanks to you, Your Majesty, our once and always beloved Green Queen Mum.

DOUBLE CROSS

There was still a great view over the river, but it had been thirty years since I'd last been there and it was no surprise that the bar seemed different from the one I remembered. When we were students we all came here after a game and even after our friends moved on and only Max and I were left we still drank here. It was a special place for us.

When we graduated there were good reasons why we went our separate ways but we swore that whatever happened we would meet in this place to the day, thirty years after we parted for good. And if there was one thing about us we always kept our promises. So there I was in the same place where we sat and hatched plans for the future all that time ago, and I guessed it must have been twenty-five years since we'd even exchanged a Christmas card.

I looked around but the place was empty, except for an attractive middle-aged, well-groomed woman, sitting with her back to me at the bar, sipping a gin and tonic and smoking a long American cigarette. She seemed slightly out of place there but there was something familiar about her that I couldn't quite put my finger on. But when she turned round the penny dropped, and my stomach lurched. It couldn't be anyone else. It was Max! My old rugby-playing, beer-drinking, joke telling friend. I didn't know what to do, and the shock must have shown on my face for she smiled and laughed. That familiar old smile. That familiar old laugh.

'Hallo Charlie,' she said. 'Long time, no see. Come over and give me a kiss, darling.' And when I'd done that, she smoothed her dress down, crossed her long legs, smiled and leaned forward.

'Bit of a turn-up for the books, isn't it?' she said and every time she spoke or laughed she was more and more the Max I'd known. Although we had much to talk about, we kept it short for we both knew we'd never meet again. With our different lives it was best to leave the past where it belonged.

'How did it go?' asked my partner, when I got home, in time to kiss the kids goodnight. 'Did you recognise each other?'

'Yes, but we'd both changed,' I said. 'We got on well enough, but we won't be seeing each other again.'

My partner must have guessed that was only part of the story because I'd made no secret of how much I'd changed in later life. But what I didn't let on was that when we were students Max had a regular girlfriend. And that girlfriend was me.

MUM'S THE WORD

'Keep mum, there's a war on,' they're always saying that to us but on the bus yesterday there were these two women sitting in front of me talking really loudly as if they didn't care who heard them. Mind you, there was only me there behind them and nobody takes much notice of me.

'I've got some news, Marge,' says Edna this woman with a greasy looking hat held in place with a big hatpin. 'They're laying off people at my Bert's firm, but an "opportunity" came up for him.'

'What sort of opportunity?' said the other one we village kids used to call "Mangy Marge". 'Wish I'd get one of those, my Jack's gone nearly three years.'

I often don't get what I think are called "nuances" and I think I missed something there, but not grasping what was going on didn't matter because Edna wasn't listening and just went on talking. I get a lot of that from people and I think it's a bit rude, although I don't like to say anything. But I hear all sorts of things being quiet and just *listening*.

'It's all very hush-hush,' Edna says, looking a bit furtive and lowering her voice. 'All he'll say is that they're working underground. But I'll have it out of him, when he's had a bit to drink and is keen on you know what.'

Marge scratched her head and looked under her fingernails for a bit.

85

'Maybe he's doin' some mining, like them Bevan boys.'

'At his age?' says Edna, a bit sharpish. 'And him a time-served electrician. "Essential war work", more like.'

'How long's all this going on?' Marge moans. 'My Jack should be home helping me with six kids, and no running water in the house. "You try keeping them clean", I said to that bloke from the council who came round because some busybody saw the state they was in. Me with a husband in a German POW camp, lounging about all day.'

As I said I never grasp half of what people say and Edna seemed to have the same problem because she still just went on talking.

'The last few days he's come home with his working shoes and trousers all white and clammy,' she said. 'Like he'd been brushin' up against a chalky wall in a tunnel or suchlike.'

'No chalk round here,' says Marge, scratching her face while poking some stray hair into her hairnet. 'Does he go off early of a morning?'

'Same as usual,' says Edna. 'So it must be somewhere round here.'

'Now I come to think of it,' says Marge. 'There was some workings down by the river, near that big quarry. When we was nippers we used to ride our bikes there and the tyres got all white and sticky. Took us ages to get it off.'

'Could be there.'

'My mother said, "Don't you go traipsing around the house with that stuff on your shoes",' says Marge. 'She used to go on something rotten about the state of my room when I was at home. It was always: "You'll never find yourself a nice young man, if you go on being such a slattern".'

'That quarry's the only place that fits the bill,' says Edna. 'Wonder what they're doing there, all them skilled men.'

'Exciting, just like a murder mystery ain't it.'

'There was this plan thing I found in his wallet wot looked like a picture of an aireo-plane.'

'Like them flying about from that RAF Airfield down Waltham way?' says Marge smearing on some lipstick, which went all over her cheek when the bus lurched.

'No, them planes have got two wings on 'em, one above the other like they should,' says Edna. 'But in the picture the aireo-plane only had one wing.'

'Don't be daft.'

'I mean one wing on either side of the plane.'

'How can that fly then?' Marge says, all scornful. 'They need four wings – two on either side, don't they? Stands to reason, they wouldn't have them if they didn't need 'em!'

'Well this had only one,' says Edna. 'And another thing, there wasn't one of them things wot whizzes around.'

'You mean a perpreller? Well that's just plain daft, too. 'Ow can you have an areo-plane with not enough wings, and no perpreller?'

'Beat's me,' says Edna, gathering up her shopping. 'Anyhow, here we are, at the stop. Now don't forget wot I've told you is strictly for your ears.'

'Don't worry, dear, "mum's the word",' says Marge. 'Ain't that Mrs Allsop down there at the stop, who's no better than she should be, what with her Fred away and that lodger of hers always around! I'll get off like you and a word with her if it's all the same to you, Edna.'

★ ★ ★

It was another two stops before I met my friend, Henry. He's really nice and so good looking! I think he'd like to be my boyfriend, but I don't really know what he does, and he's a bit cagey about that, probably on account of him having once had a name like Muller. I saw it written on an envelope addressed to him when he said he was living in Holland before the war. He's "Miller" now, and not like the other boys who're only after one thing because he seems interested in all the local gossip. So I couldn't wait to tell him bits of what I'd heard on the bus, and I hope it'll make him like me even more. And if I promise to tell him everything like that in the future maybe, I'll learn a bit more about him and some of his friends.

And after *that,* my dear *Herr* Muller, my real boyfriend and his pals from Special Branch will be round to have a little word with you and your mates. Marge and Enid too I wouldn't be surprised, after I spill the beans about them. But "Mum's the Word" – it doesn't do to trust anyone these days, does it?

THE LAST WALTZ

'`ve always had to be careful about money, but it wasn't as if I was hard up or anything like that when I eventually got the news. I suppose we could all do with a bit more money but somehow it was all too late. And as I said after I'd heard from the solicitor I really didn't need *that* much. Does that make sense? Sorry if it doesn't, I know I ramble on a bit at times. Anyway, I didn't think much about it at the time because I had other things on my mind although what they were now I've no idea.

I remember always feeling distracted and "dithery" round about then and never really getting *round to things* if you know what I mean. My doctor called it "Age Related Attention Deficit Syndrome". I thought she should have come out with the real reason and just say: "you're a frightened old lady who forgets things because you're not coping well on your own and fearful for your future". And that would be true because everything was moving and changing so quickly, and younger people didn't make allowances for you being slow and no one seemed to *care* anymore. I meant to look up the word "syndrome" in case it meant something awful but never got round to it.

Anyway, I must hurry up and say that I was getting ready about that time to go on holiday. Just me. So I got my suitcase down from the shelf in the cupboard under the stairs and was wondering as usual why I always left it too late to buy another in a sale. Mine was so battered and heavy to carry that when at last I'd plucked up enough courage to go on a holiday it was always in a coach with a lot of strange people, and I was the only one lugging my case around because it didn't have wheels. Wat a good idea they are!

But I've always tried to be honest and the real reason I didn't get a new one was because I hoped some nice gentleman on the coach would help me with the case and it might help to break the ice. I smiled and tried to be friendly to the others but it still got a bit lonely on my own with all those couples on the coach. The marrieds were the worst! It never seemed to matter how long they'd been together or how decrepit the husband looked the wives always held on to them like limpets. The glares I've had! It's really more to do with how the women had let themselves go and not kept themselves looking nice. Perhaps they never bothered making an effort after they'd got their man when they were still young and pretty.

Where was I? After I found the suitcase, I carried it into the lounge and began looking for a duster to clean it with. I never seem to put things back in the same place so I'm always looking for them. Keeps me busy though – you must be positive in this life! I keep dusters in a box of rags under the stairs along with my magazines. I didn't like to throw away the back-numbers and all my old shoes were there too. There must have been dozens in that cupboard! One day I'd promised myself I was going to have a really great time looking at all those shoes that I was given as presents or saved up to buy. I remember I wanted them so much and now here they were all hidden away and unused.

There were shoes I wanted to wear to dances in the Church Hall, but never did, tap dancing pumps and ballet shoes all still in their new wrappings. I was quite small when they found out I'd got polio, but I yearned to have shoes to wear when I got better and could walk and dance like other people. It never happened and I had to make the best of it – which I've always tried to do.

And now the shoes look so nice and new that I wish I had an excuse to wear them now, not that they'd fit my old feet! But I still have the lovely thought of what fun we could have had together! Keep cheerful, that's my motto!

Then I was in such a state I thought I heard a noise at the front door and I almost ran to made sure the chain and lock were fastened. A friend of mine, more of an acquaintance really, answered her front door and it was pushed open by a man come to sell her an insurance policy. And he wouldn't take no for an answer and she bought one that turned out to be worthless, and she'd been paying premiums for years before she found out. So I always lock my front door and I had a little spyhole made to look through.

I would have used it but I wasn't really tall enough to see who was there unless I climbed on a stool from the kitchen. The one with the leg that sometimes came loose. I never wanted children but sometimes I feel I'd like to have had a strong son who could mend things like that stool. Whatever they say young people can be very thoughtful helping people like me across the road or giving up a seat in the bus. And as for paying bills – they always got into such a mess – I never knew where to go for help and it made me feel so helpless and lonely. I'd find myself crying all alone, and that made it feel even worse. Then I say: "Come on Dolly, chin up girl!" and I'd grin and have a cup of tea.

Once a man wanting work shouted he had come to mend the roof and kept on knocking at the door. I stood there in the hall wondering who it was, and then I hit on a plan. "Always *do* something when you're afraid," I've always said. I could get the stool and look out or be very quiet like a mouse and hope that however was there would go away. When we were little my sister and I used to play at being quiet as mice, but if we were a bit noisy my mother would shout at us and threaten to tell our father. But really she was scared of him because he shouted at her and used to hit her, too. We were very quiet when he'd done that

91

and we'd pretend that it hadn't happened and that we were in a happy family like the ones we read about in our children's books. I loved to play with my sister but when I got sick and went to hospital she was sent away and lived with a foster mum. I didn't see much of her after that, and I really wanted to because I was on my own with these strange people and my leg hurt so. And it was really hard to stay cheery and bright and my mum hardly came to see me at all.

Then the postie did come and instead of the usual rubbish, which is all I ever get, there was a very posh looking letter with a rather grand solicitors name and address on the back, but I was in such a state about the packing that I didn't bother just then with opening it. To be truthful I forgot all about it because of being worried about catching the feeder bus as they call it which was to pick me up next morning. The next day I was ready hours before I needed to be and when I heard the bus drawing up outside, I picked up my suitcase and ran down the drive with it. And then the catch came loose and some of my clothes spilled on the ground. I got really upset picking them up because I knew we might miss the main coach, and the other passengers weren't very nice to me except one older gentleman who had a twinkle in his eye and got down out of the bus and helped me get the things into the case and then me into the bus.

'Don't you worry about them, my dear,' he said. 'You can sit next to me and stop me feeling lonely.' And he looked after me for the whole holiday, and being a couple felt like rejoining the human race because of the different way people treated me. It was the best ever. And he didn't seem to notice my limp which has always stopped me getting to know people. Men, I mean.

Wasn't that nice of him? Then I found the letter just scrumpled up and shoved into my pocket as I left the house.

'What's that you've got there, Dottie-Dolly,' said Ted – that was the name of the nice gentleman, and what he called me. Cheeky thing.

'Haven't opened it yet.'

'I'll tell you what,' says Ted, 'Let's both look and see what it says.'

As the address on the envelope suggested it was from some solicitor in a posh part of London which made me so anxious I could hardly open it. My hands were all of a tremble and Ted helped me take out the letter – all on very stiff paper and smelling really *expensive,* if you know what I mean.

'Does the name Forbes-Robinson mean anything, Dolly dear,' said Ted, gently. He might tease me but he's really very *protective*. I love that.

'No,' I said.

'First name Amelia?' he said. 'Ring a bell?'

'Yes, yes – Mellie, Mellie!' I said. 'I used to help out cleaning in the big house as we called it and Mellie was their only child. We were such pals and used to go for walks in the park when I'd finished my cleaning chores. And one day when this horrible dog attacked her I was badly bitten trying to keep it away from her and had to have these horrible injections in my tummy.'

'One day, Dollie,' she said to me, when she saw me in hospital, 'I'll repay you for saving me like that.' But then she was sent off to boarding school, and although we kept writing to each other for years and years we lost touch when she married and moved to South Africa. I hope nothing's happened to her.'

Well, what had happened is that she had died and in her will she had instructed her solicitor to get some people to track me down and tell me that she had left me some money and a nice little house – more a flat really, in a place called Cheyne Walk.

★ ★ ★

I didn't need the flat and Ted helped me get a good price for it. Good price indeed! I couldn't believe such a tiny place was worth so much! Not to mention the money – a very "tidy sum" as we'd call it in my day. All I know is I was a bit set in my ways to let it all change my life much. And it wouldn't compensate for my sister not being around when I needed her, or my mum getting a beating or my dad not getting punished for what he did to us. Or mend my leg or make up for all those lonely days and nights I'd had for most of my life. But what it could do was stop some of those things happening to others, and if it could they were welcome to it.

And Ted had a bit put aside since his wife died, and he said he didn't want a penny of my winnings. And although we haven't had long to be happy together, we've made the most of it by spending the money on kids in hospital, hostels for abused women and research into cancer. Ted's wife died of cancer and now I've got it. Just my luck!

But I feel more alive than ever and we're going to live every day. And I'll go on squeezing into my dancing shoes and the two of us, silly old people that we are, will go on dancing together in front of the electric fire. And Victor Sylvester and his orchestra will be on the old gramophone and I know dear Ted will be there to hold my hand when the time comes for us to dance the Last Waltz together.

Did you notice that I used the word "together?" It's one I've wanted to say all my life about someone I care for and who cares for me. And it's been worth the wait, every minute of it, even now. I expect you think that's just daft. Well just for once, you can think exactly what you like!

THE SIXPENCE

My uncle was well off when he died but chose to live as if in poverty most of his life and at the inquest, after he'd been found dead in bed clutching a roll of banknotes, I described his lifestyle as "frugal" and that fitted him well. He was born in 1915 and worked in accountancy both before and after his years in the Middle East during the Second World War.

Some men covet stamps or cigarette cards, one I knew collected vacuum cleaners and another irons. My uncle felt the same way about money. But I never thought of him as a miser – he just liked having money but not spending it. He had few material needs, not many possessions and no interest at all in his domestic environment. He'd lived in the same house for eighty years, with no hot water, bathroom or central heating and to get to the outside privy you had to clamber over the collapsed ruins of the garden shed.

In 1933 he began keeping a diary in which he wrote every day for sixty years. Most entries were brief and factual and if you thought so much clear writing about your daily doings must reveal *something* about the author you'd be wrong in his case. Like Shakespeare he wasn't letting on. But one brief entry did catch my eye.

As you might expect he was careful where and how he shopped. And one day he noted in his diary that he'd found sixpence on the floor of the local Co-op. I doubt he kept it to himself for he was scrupulously honest. But I suspect it was such a small sum even then that the management probably laughed at his honesty and told him to keep it. In any case it was the finding he recorded with pleasure suggesting to me that he probably saved it.

I recall my surprise at him even bothering to record such a trivial incident, and I was sad at the thought of a greedy old man coveting so little. But I was so young. Now I'm older and live at a time when people need to possess more and more in their unending search for status and happiness and I feel how lucky he was to feel so pleased when all it took was finding a sixpence!

A SHADE TO THE RIGHT

f you think "selfies" are new, pandering to modern kids' narcissism you'd be wrong, for I was taking them years ago. I'd set my camera to automatic, put it on a tripod and then take my picture. But only when I was in some interesting place or situation and never to show me with my "five-minute" mates or record that hilarious party when everyone got drunk before everything was ruined by what happened afterwards. And I was too honest to use a photograph to pretend I was someone I wasn't, or felt what I didn't feel, or owned things I didn't possess.

But I've always liked keeping *records* of things and I suppose I didn't like the idea of my life just sliding away into oblivion, unrecorded. And so, after I'd taken them, I hardly looked at most of the photos because I wanted to store them up and look at them all together later in my life One day I said to myself when I felt the time was right they would remind me of all the places and things that were a part of making me, *me*. Showing how I'd changed as the years went by, growing more lined, smiling less or more, getting fatter and losing youthful freshness along with the hair.

And that brings me to last Tuesday, the day I decided I shouldn't delay looking at them any longer. My wife wasn't interested and I waited until she was out shopping before climbing up to the attic and bringing down all the boxes containing the photos. Then I sat down in what I call my study and my wife the laundry room with the collection of photos all arranged by date and began to go through them.

The early ones were mildly interesting seeing different hairstyles and clothes, meetings with forgotten people and some dull places. Why on Earth would I want to record being on a Belgium autobahn in late Autumn? But as the years went by and the panorama of my life moved before me I saw something that first puzzled, then annoyed and finally worried me.

In the very early photos there was an indistinct shadow in the background, which I put down to poor equipment or my inexperience with the camera. But as the years went by and in spite of better kit and my improved skills, the shadow stayed always behind me and to my right. And although too *elusive* to describe, it seemed to *change* in texture and shape over time becoming more patchy and less symmetrical.

I couldn't account for a shape appearing so consistently in so many places, using different equipment over such a long period and however much I squinted at it I got no further than making out a cylindrical blob, roughly my height of about six feet. But what concerned me most, was that over time this indistinct image was getting closer to me. When I showed some of these photos to a friend, he said it reminded him of the sequence in the film *The Omen* when the priest is killed by something appearing as a shadow shaped like a sword on photos of him before he died. Half joking my friend suggested I consult a priest.

And I was so worried that I went to the local church and found the local Catholic priest in the sacristy sorting out some vestments. I explained the problem and he put me in contact with a colleague of his who specialised in spiritual matters of this sort. And that's how I met Father O'Donnell in the seminary where he lived, taking a small glass of sherry with some lady parishioners. Irish, dark haired, with ivory skin the texture of parchment, he was eager to help with what he sensed was a rare serious enquiry. I showed him a few of the photos over the years and he asked me questions about me and my life. "Suburban, dull and ordinary" was the usual assessment of me by Freda my wife, which I duly passed on.

'Any idea what the shadow might be?' I asked him.

'Do you believe in Guardian Angels?'

'I don't know,' I said. 'I've never given them much thought. Why? Do you think it's one of those?'

'Could be yours,' he said. 'Technically, we refer to them as "shades".'

'Why would this "shade" move nearer to me?'

'Perhaps it wants to tell you something,' he said. 'Only an idea.'

'How would I know if it does?'

'Ask it. Find somewhere quiet tonight and hear what it has to say.'

'Is that it, Father?' I said. 'No incantations, bells and whistles. You rather go in for that sort of thing don't you?'

'If that's all, Mr Thomas,' he said, 'Let me know how you get on.'

★ ★ ★

My wife was out again that evening and I sat quietly in the living room and feeling rather silly I said, 'Guardian Angel can you hear me?'

'No need to shout,' said a voice which seemed to be in my ear but it was hard to tell.

'Do you want to tell me something?'

'Not particularly,' said the voice, in a pleasant but rather indifferent way. 'I'm Rodney, by the way.'

'*Rodney*?' I said. 'What exactly is it that you do?'

'I guard you.'

'From what?'

'Yourself usually.'

'Is that it?'

'Yes, more or less. Yes.'

'How?'

'I'm your conscience.'

'Are you dead?'

'No of course not. I'd have to have lived to be dead. I'm an *Angel*.'

'What happens to you when I die?'

'No idea – I'm new to all this,' said the voice. 'Another thing to worry about, I suppose. Thank you so very much.'

'Why are you in so many of my photos?'

'It shows how we "developed" together,' said Rodney with a chuckle at the awful pun. 'Seriously though, as we grew older it was only natural we got closer to each other, and the images capture that rather well, don't you think?'

'I didn't feel close to you in the past nor do I now,' I said. 'And another thing I can't say I warmed to the way your shape and colour changed as time went on. Are you ill, or something?'

'Funny, you said that,' he said, sounding concerned. 'Can you be more specific? About the shape, I mean, and the colour.'

'Well, you started off all bright, smooth and symmetrical – like an elongated yellow egg. And then...'

'And then what? Don't stop now.'

'Well, you got dimmer and more... *battered*.'

'I knew it, I knew it. I should never have gone on that holiday with you to Botswana.'

'What happened?'

'I don't want to talk about it, but there are some very scary spirits around the bush in the Okavanga that you don't want sneaking-up on you when you're *guarding*,' his voice trembled.

'When I heard you were planning to go there I told them I wasn't ready for it. *"You'll be alright on your own,"* they said. So, guarding it was, and I'd barely got my wings.'

'I'd like to help, but I don't know where to start.'

'Just *be* there for me in an unguarded moment,' he said. 'I've a big test coming up involving some heavy-duty protection.'

'I can't produce an unguarded moment, just like that,' I said. 'Especially now I'm on my guard.'

'Boo!'

'That was pathetic,' I said, 'I wasn't remotely unguarded.'

He stopped speaking after that.

I don't remember being particularly concerned about the situation, but I went back to see Father O'Donnell who was stocktaking in the vestry. He looked up from the communion wine cupboard and, when I told him what had happened, he smiled oddly. He then carefully locked the door of the cupboard and after telling me to follow him climbed up some narrow stone steps to the flat roof of the tower above the churchyard far below.

'Go over to the battlement there, my son,' he said pointing. 'And look down and tell me what you see,' he said.

I walked over to the low wall and peered cautiously over the edge.

'I don't see anything unusual, down there,' I said.

'Move a little to the right, dear boy,' he said. 'Where the parapet's a bit lower.'

I did as he suggested and he then pushed me over the low wall and I plummeted soundlessly down to fall heavily amongst the gravestones.

★ ★ ★

To give him his due the Father was one of my first visitors in the hospital with some lovely flowers and a sampler woven by one of his ladies to celebrate my fall.

'Well, and how are you today,' he said cheerfully. 'Plaster coming off the leg tomorrow I hear. A happy day and all the better for your miraculous recovery.'

'Happy day!' I almost shouted. 'You pushed me off a church tower and I broke my ankle. What's happy about that?'

'Rodney passed his test with flying colours,' he replied. 'An anxious time for him but a joyous outcome indeed.'

'Oh, I am pleased,' I said. 'How I look forward to more of his so-called guardianship. What will it be for me next – a broken neck or complete paralysis?'

'You do him a sad misjustice, I fear,' said the Father. 'He had every right to go off duty but wanted to stay with you as long as possible.'

'Go off duty? I thought he was on duty 24/7 for the whole of my natural life!'

'Indeed,' said the Priest. 'But he was aware that later that day you were due be run over by a No 22 bus and you would therefore no longer need his services.'

'So why wasn't I run over by the bus?'

'Rodney had previously interceded on your behalf and offered to prove to his examiners that he was fully capable of protecting you,' said O'Donnell. 'Almost a perfect score on slowing your descent but for the slight glitch at its conclusion. And of course, now you still have your life ahead of you with a more *seasoned* Guardian Angel.'

'But what if he'd failed to cushion my fall or whatever he did to save me?'

'Then you would merely have met your preordained destiny of dying but in a different way,' said the Father. 'Quite neat really.'

A familiar voice, now strong and triumphant, rang out in my ears. 'How's that for guarding?' it said.

'Well done, Rodney,' I said. 'And thanks for catching me when I fell.'

'It was nothing,' he said.

'I'm so pleased you appreciate what the young shade has done for you,' said Father O'Donnell. 'And given that it was your camera work that revealed him to you in the first place, I took the liberty of asking your wife to loan us your camera for a celebratory picture.'

'And a good time for a selfie,' I said, putting my camera on a table in front of my bed, with the priest on my right leaning towards me.

'Make sure you get my best side,' said Rodney.

'Then *incline* towards me a fraction,' I said to him on the other side. 'And a "shade to the right," to borrow the good Father's last words to me before my fall and your elevation. "Cheese!" everyone!'

THE PROBLEM WITH GOD

M any years ago, I invited my favourite niece to lunch and was waiting for her in the foyer of the hotel where we were to dine. In those days she was often late for appointments, and I found a magazine on a nearby table to read while I was waiting for her. In it I found an article about the life of those who manned Hadrian's Wall in the second century during the Pax Romana. And what I found most intriguing was evidence regarding Roman attitudes and behaviour towards their personal Gods whose help they sought through prayer and offerings.

It seemed that those deities who came up with the goods were retained but those who failed to respond were dropped in favour of more "accommodating" rivals. I was reflecting on this pragmatic approach to religion when there was a mild disturbance by the revolving doors and into the lobby burst my niece in her customary whirlwind of frantic apology. We went in to lunch at once and I asked her how she was.

'Gosh!' she said, 'I'm so happy!'

'I'm pleased to hear it. What's making you feel like that?'

'God, you know,' she said quietly, modestly lowering her eyes. 'It's like having a chum you can talk to whenever you want, about anything really. Well, perhaps not *absolutely* everything but pretty close to it. And someone who understands just everything about you.' She gave a little giggle and beamed at me through the severe round glasses she'd adopted since she'd joined the "Circle of Light".

I suggested we might have a bottle of wine with our lunch.

'Gosh, terrific,' she said. 'But not too much – after two glasses or so I get quite squiffy.'

'Well we can drink it slowly,' I said, and she burst into a spasm of hearty guffawing.

She was so full of animal high spirits, enthusiastic and quite guileless that I found it impossible not to wish her well. And we left on the best of terms, promising to stay in contact in the future.

We didn't meet for some months but when we did, I was surprised to find how much her appearance had altered. Her hair was now soft and long, no longer cut severely short and parted up the middle. She was wearing make-up and as her glasses had disappeared I assumed she was now using modern contact lenses. But she still exuded energy and optimism and after exchanging family gossip I asked her about God.

'Gosh, you know I kept asking and asking him for things and nothing ever happened! Nothing! So I gave him up. Silly old God!'

'Hasn't that left a bit of a hole in your life?' I asked.

'A bit at first – but I'm playing tennis really seriously now instead of going to church. I play really well. It's great if you get down in the dumps. Do you play? Would you like a game sometime?'

DEJA VU

I
f Tony hadn't left the maps he'd bought in Stanfords, the well-
known travel bookshop, he wouldn't have met the person who
was to influence his whole life. Perhaps a meeting somewhere
was inevitable. Who can tell? Anyway, five minutes after
leaving the shop he had the familiar feeling that he'd forgotten
something and had just worked out it must be the maps when
this very attractive young lady approached him *She must think I'm
someone else, the lucky blighter,* he thought. How could he guess the
fortunate fellow was him?

'Excuse me,' she said, 'I was behind you in the queue in the
bookshop and you left your maps on the counter. The assistant
couldn't leave the shop so I said I'd see where you'd gone and
give them to you. And now I've found you and here they are.'

She smiled and gave him the package and he smiled back
thinking *and here you are too!* His heart was thumping like
mad which it went on doing over the coffee he bought her to
celebrate. In his experience things like that didn't happen very
often to people in London and never to absent-minded idiots
like him. But nice as the encounter was proving to be it had its
unsettling side too. For it turned out she'd bought the same maps
as him. *Exactly* the same.

What was so strange was that the two Ordinance Survey
charts they'd chosen covered a rural part of Herefordshire and

were large scale containing a large amount of detail within a small area. Another odd thing thinking about it later was just what had prompted him to decide to spend time in such an unfamiliar part of the country. And it seemed that Polly, the lovely girl, was thinking along similar lines although she said she'd be going there with her boyfriend.

A *boyfriend* he thought, sullen clouds darkening the light shining down on what might be a heaven-sent relationship. *With someone as attractive as her what did he expect?* In fact he was marvelling at their having coffee at all for he was no oil painting – an observation from a friend he could well have done without. Well at least he'd been able to smirk at the no-hopers throwing envious glances in his direction for being with such a good looker!

Then things got even better as if he was in a delicious dream that wasn't going to end. For it seemed she actually liked them being together and the more they chatted the more they enjoyed it. Only much later did it occur to him how unusual it was that two strangers found so much to say to one another so soon after meeting. They talked all morning and then lunched together even though she had arranged to meet her boyfriend.

'He's stood me up enough times, and now it's my turn,' she said. 'Anyway, he's on the way out and if you don't mind I'll use you as an excuse to get rid of him.'

Don't mind! he thought. *You must be joking!*

In the event neither of them got to Herefordshire as they planned and life began moving a lot faster for him than before they met. And in spite of his delight in their relationship he always felt they were *right* together and her good looks, although a wonderful bonus, were not the primary cause of their closeness. A fact she'd recognised long before him. And it was she who drove the bus with him the sole passenger careering down the road to end in marriage a few months later.

So why did they feel like that from the very beginning? One reason was they shared a deep affinity for the early 1950s. Not really surprising with them both being born in the late 30s and growing up in the same period but it was much deeper than simple nostalgia for a vanished era. There again there was a shared feeling that they'd known each other before they met and the common bond of both being adopted when they were about four years old.

Tony had been found wandering in Kensington Gardens and Polly had been abandoned near the Victoria and Albert Museum. Neither those who rescued them or their fosterers knew anything about their birth parents but they were rescued at a confusing time with an air raid on and the war in full swing. Any number of reasons might have accounted for their abandonment and all they knew was that neither had any recollection of life before London. In the event they were both happy with their adopted parents and grew up in comfortable circumstances in different parts of the capital.

Busy and productive years followed with Polly working as a partner in a small firm of solicitors and Tony running a literary agency specializing in the occult, supernatural and fantasy. The usual family years passed and with the children gone and them approaching sixty-five they began thinking about a different sort of life. And so they decided to spend half their time in the country to see how bucolic life might suit them, with Polly working part-time from home and Tony acting as a consultant to his agency.

That meant it was only a matter of deciding where to go and there they hit a problem. Living and working in London all their lives they scarcely knew anything about the English countryside or the people who lived in it. Was it a coincidence that they chose Herefordshire, the county which the Stanford maps had brought them together in the first place? Neither recalled their past interest in the place but liked the sound of fruit growing country thinking how *wholesome* it sounded with its healthy, natural produce, grown and gathered by sturdy yeomen aided by apple cheeked bustling wives. Real people producing authentic food with some Anglo Saxon *bottom* to it. Granny Smith apples straight from the bough, not Pedro's Promise Passion fruit from the ship's container!

'We must have an orchard,' said Polly. 'With really old trees.'

'And gnarled, mossy trunks with branches bearing mistletoe, long past fruit bearing age?'

'You get my drift,' said his wife.

'So where are these menopausal arboreals to be found?' said Tony. 'And will their scanty leaves shade us from the burning sun and not just dapple the ground with soft shadows in the cool of the evening? Will they not give sanctuary to thieving birds flocking to this fruit bearing Eden and harbour wasps getting nasty-drunk on fermented fruit?'

'You are so uncool,' said Polly, who used such horrible phrases to help whisk away negative notions.

'So let's find an orchard,' Tony said, humming a snatch from "where... the apple tree do lean down low in Linden Lea".

After a while they found one near Ledbury which they'd used as a base for finding a retreat. To their surprise Frank Lombard the local estate agent soon found them an orchard complete with just the cottage they'd been looking for. It was perfect: thatched and be-vined with the black plastic water butt and a poorly built modern lean-to, the hallmarks of rustic authenticity. And with the trees came two acres of rough pasture and a small stream.

Frank wanted no obstacles to a quick sale and reassured them about the upkeep of the grounds.

'Don't worry, a local with a few sheep will pay you to keep the pasture under control,' he said.

'Great thing this countryside,' Tony remarked. 'They pay you to do things you don't want to do.'

'Just one thing,' said Frank rather too casually. 'If you visit the village don't take any notice of gossip about the late owner.'

'Was there a problem?'

'Not really – it belonged to old Mother Walsh,' he said. 'She'd lived in the cottage for donkey's years and was well into her 90s when she died. The older villagers still see her as a witch because of the way she acted after a family tragedy.'

'Surely, not in this day and age,' said Tony.

'You'll find old wives tales linger longer than that in the country round here,' said Frank.

'What tragedy?'

'It involved her son Michael,' he said. 'He was *different* from the local lads and they bullied him so much she took him away from the local school. He'd probably be classified as autistic these days, but boys will be boys and he was treated very badly.'

'Was he sent away?'

'Who knows?' said Frank. 'It was years ago and things got… overlooked.'

'So he might have been at home?'

'Wherever he was he wasn't seen for many years around these parts and when he did turn up no one was going to tease him for he was a huge chap with a black beard driving a battered, old car. He'd career around the lanes at great speed and everyone looked out when he was at the wheel and it was that which led to the tragedy.'

'What happened?'

'A family used to come down from London for the summer with two kids, a boy and a girl. They were inseparable, always wandering about together, and got on well with the village kids even though they came from a much better-off family. Then one day they went out exploring and didn't come back.'

'Ever?' said Polly.

'Never seen again,' said Frank. 'All the village knew was that Michael was driving around about the time they were out and they put two and two together.'

'And it came to more than four.'

'This is the country! Anyway, he was suspected but never convicted of running them over and getting rid of the bodies. His mother hotly denied it and nothing was ever proved one way or the other.'

'How did the village take it?'

'Very badly. The devastated families involved were well liked and the village made life hell for both of them. So much so, that Michael committed suicide. No one went to the funeral except old Mother Walsh dressed all in black, and after the ceremony she swept into the bar of the local and screamed and hissed at the villagers who avoided her stare.

'Curse you all,' she shouted. 'Them kids'll come back the pair of them. And then you'll see he's innocent, and he'll have the laugh on you! And now keep off my land the whole part and parcel of you, or I'll set the dogs on you!'

'What a dreadful story,' said Polly.

'Anything we should know about the conditions of sale?' Tony asked to lighten the mood and move on.

'When the old lady died, still dressed in black, a distant cousin inherited the property,' said Frank. 'As far as I know he hasn't even visited it but he wants to honour her stipulation about keeping the cottage and the grounds together.'

'So that's why we got the orchard,' said Tony.

They kept a small flat in London but settled in well enough in the cottage although the older villagers gave them some odd looks. And to get to know them better Tony went to the local pub for lunch but found only one very old man in the bar hunched over a pint.

'We've moved into Twelvetrees Cottage,' Tony said, sitting down near him.

'Took yer time,' the old man said, looking into his beer mug.

'I don't know what you mean?' said Tony.

'I'll bid you good-day,' the man said, pushing his half-full mug away and shoving back his seat. He got up and went out without a further word.

'Did I say something to upset him?' said Tony to Henry the landlord, polishing glasses.

'Couldn't say, Sir,' he said, replacing the glasses and beginning to walk to the other end of the bar.

'What did he mean about my taking my time?'

'Speaks out of turn, old George, should know better,' he said. 'No sense raking up the past, leave it be.'

'We've no past to rake up.'

'As you say,' he said. 'But folk get things stuck in their heads.'

'What things?'

'Last orders now, Sir,' he said, moving off.

'What did you make of that?' Polly said when he told her what had happened.

'No idea, but I'm not going in there again,' said Tony.

They never did and just lived quietly, working hard in the day, shopping outside the village and sitting in the orchard in the evenings when the weather was good. In spite of what the agent had said they found it impossible to find anyone prepared to let their animals graze on their land and just left it neglected.

'What do you call it when you walk around the limits of your property?' Polly said when they were having a sundowner in the gathering dusk of a warm, early October evening.

'Beating the bounds.'

'No point in knowing that if you don't put it into practice,' she said.

'No time like the present,' he replied.

They trudged through the long grass where the ground sloped sharply down towards the little stream and discovered an overgrown track clearly unused for many years. Hidden away at the end of it was a ramshackle wooden shed with a half-collapsed roof partly propped up by something inside. Pushing open the rotten doors Tony found a tarpaulin had been roughly dragged over something and tied down with ropes. Judging from its condition both the covering and what it protected had lain undisturbed for many years. He pulled the tarp away and saw that the car underneath it with a dented front wing and a buckled number plate was a 1950s Wolseley12/48.

'You've gone white,' said Polly.

'It's an old car, and it's been in an accident.'

'So what?'

'This place gives me the creeps,' he said. 'And finding this car doesn't help. What's worse this orchard has a familiar feeling about it.'

'Déjà vu?' laughed Polly. 'But I know what you mean. I feel the same about that strange dip in the meadow down there, surrounded by the old apple trees.

'You'll think it weird,' she said after they'd made their way to the spot through thigh-high grass. 'But I know if we look at the bark on the trees here we'll find some old carvings.'

'Like initials.'

'Yes,' said Polly, in an odd voice. 'Look here's something.'

'They're old and grown over,' he said.

'But they're here, aren't they?' she said stroking the rough bark. 'I just *knew* it.'

'Lots of these old trees might have things carved on them,' Tony said, sounding as unconvincing as he felt.

'*Our* initials, I'll bet,' Polly said softly.

'That's just silly,' Tony said, unconvinced. 'And there are lots of others here as well. Village kids, most likely.'

'I really can't stay here a moment longer,' said Polly, 'The country doesn't work for us, and no one wants us here. I *hate* it.'

'All right,' said Tony, who felt the same. 'I agree it's best we call it a day. I'll ring Frank first thing in the morning and put the cottage back on the market.' *Next we'll end up seeing the old witch,* he thought.

They began climbing up the hill in the darkening dusk and coming towards in the gloom were two dark figures – an old woman in black holding the arm of a bearded giant with his head back bellowing with laughter.

'Mrs. Walsh's promise to her dead son to have the last laugh,' Polly quavered.

Tony grabbed her hand and to their later shame they took to their heels and drove straight to London.

★ ★ ★

'Mother Hoskins was out with her boy the other last night,' said old George to Henry the publican in the bar. 'Took a short cut through the Londoners' land and nigh scared the buggers to death. Bolted like scared rabbits, the pair of 'em.'

'She didn't mean no harm,' said Henry. 'Her Tom might be a bit soft in the head but he wouldn't hurt a fly. He's as gentle as a baby.'

'Just looks like that Hagrid bloke on the telly,' said George. 'That's all.'

'Cottage up for sale again shouldn't wonder,' said Henry. 'Had my eye on that for years, but the likes of them puts the price up so much I can't get a look in. My bet is now they've gone for good.'

'Not so sure about that,' said George. 'You're too young to know what happened with that old witch. And something *unnatural* about them bein' man and wife. There's more to come, you'll see.'

'What sort of something?'

'Unfinished business, sort of something,' said George, getting up to go home. 'You mark my words they'll be back.'

The landlord didn't agree, but George was right about the unfinished business.

★ ★ ★

Tony and Polly lay in bed in the London flat each in a tight, separate cocoon of discomfort.

'I wish to God we hadn't gone there,' said Tony.

'How were we to know?' said Polly in a small, miserable voice. 'It's so unfair.'

'Do we tell the kids?' said Tony, the question they'd both been dreading.

'What good would that do?' said Polly. 'Just spread the pain around more that's all.'

'I don't feel any different,' said Tony, 'I mean different than before.'

'Of course, it's *different* from before and you know it is,' she cried, beginning to sob.

'What we did was only wrong if we knew what we were doing,' he said fiercely, but there was no reply.

★ ★ ★

The next prospective owner of the cottage saw two small mounds both overlooked by Tony and Polly in the hollow near the trees where generations of villagers had carved their initials. Intrigued he had them dug up before he proceeded with the sale, and inside were two small skeletons, which forensic analysis confirmed were the bodies of siblings.

Since putting the cottage on the market Tony and Polly had never been near the village, and when the sale was over, they had decided, heartbroken, to go their separate ways. On the very day they were about to part for ever, Tony had a call from Frank the agent who'd handled the sale and was finalising the deal.

'Seems the mystery about the two dead kids has been solved,' he said, explaining about the graves and the skeletons of the dead children.

'Hold on a moment.' said Tony. 'I want to tell my wife what you've just told me. She'll be happy to hear that.'

And she was, she really was.

BEYOND THE REACH OF STORMS

From the moment he arrived, elderly and ill, he was a puzzle to the staff of the hostel near the railway arches in Vauxhall. Largely because he had about him an unusual gentleness that a casual glance at his dishevelled clothes and gaunt, unshaven face would never have detected or suspected.

The staff learned that his name was John and judging from his burr, though hardened through many years at sea among strangers, it seemed likely that he came from Cornwall. The doctor diagnosed him as being just about on the healthy side of not requiring hospital treatment but both he and the experienced staff could see the signs of what was coming and made him as comfortable as they could.

In another world of opportunity he'd have been in a hospice surrounded by kith and kin, but here he was alone. There was no one he wished staff to contact on his behalf, and he avoided close contact with other people, except for one of the hostel's visitors.

Irene was a volunteer helper, herself from a Cornwall fishing village, who radiated goodwill which she dispensed with impartial generosity to everyone in the hostel but had a special feeling for the old seaman. They both knew his time was coming and he spoke softly to her, reassured by their common links with the sea and the far west where shadows were long and the sun seldom shone directly overhead.

Leslie Grant the manager asked her to inquire again if there was anyone they might contact now the end was getting ever nearer.

'There's no one left,' said Irene. 'And he's been alone for many years without being lonely or having a shred of self pity.'

'Has he told you anything about his early life?' asked Leslie. It was quite normal for those dying alone to speak of their early life when they'd had family, friends and neighbours.

'He grew up in a remote fishing village even further west than mine,' said Irene. 'The sea's really dangerous there and his forefathers had lived by it for as long as tales had been told. He said that for generations they'd dwelt in houses huddled together in a deep damp valley between high cliffs. But there's no one there now.'

And then a little later lying in the dark holding her hand John spoke about his early life.

'My father put a light in the highest window of our home,' he said. 'It faced the sea and was to guide wayfarers on those wild waters. The angry white waves, you'll remember.'

Irene nodded and pressed his hand.

'And it was my job to mind it when I was a boy,' said John. 'Many came round to thank Dad and said without it they would never have found the harbour. It became a matter of honour for our family that the light never went out. And I never failed to keep it lit.'

'But times changed,' said Irene, and John told me that when the war came the army took over the village and all the people left for the world beyond the headland. None ever returned, the houses fell into disrepair and there was no one to tend the light.

'No one left to show them home to the harbour,' said John. 'To safe anchorage in calm water.'

The last time Irene saw him the end was very near. She held his hand and said, 'Safe passage, dear John.'

Then he squeezed her hand and whispered, 'The tide's turned, Irene, but I'm not afraid.'

Far away to the west from a window high in an empty house on a desolate shore a light appeared piercing the darkness over an angry, swelling sea. For a while it was steady but then it flickered and was gone. But not before it had guided a weary wayfarer into shelter of the harbour he knew so well, safe now and beyond the reach of storms.

A WINTER'S TRAIL

t was in late November, and I'd been staying alone in a friend's cottage near Hinton Ampner in Hampshire when I started out on my walk. It was a sparkling frosty morning and the hedgerows were white with hoar frost glistening brightly in the early morning sun. Although I was well equipped and warmly clothed, I was feeling nervous for I was no longer young and planned to walk much further than usual.

My first objective was to get to Beacon Hill from which on a clear day there was a view as far as Southampton. The journey started well for I was alone on a well-marked road with no walkers or dogs in sight. I'd been attacked by these animals in the past and always felt anxious when approaching buildings on lonely roads or farms, for country people who neither fear dogs nor understand those who do often let the animals roam freely. After an hour and a half of steady walking I reached the Hill feeling the warmth of the sun in the dry, crisp air. I felt fresh, fit, and full of walking.

I then took the path down through a smooth-shaped valley descending sharply while on my right a broad expanse of sheep-cropped down-land sloped away into the distance. Lovely, rolling well-farmed countryside. The going was easy but when I approached the bottom of the valley, I met a herd of shaggy, long-horned cattle looking aggressive and temperamental. As I could see no way of avoiding them on the path I began climbing back the way I had come. While I was climbing the path I saw a way of returning to my original route avoiding the cattle although it involved scrambling through a private pheasant shoot and squeezing through barbed wire which I found hard, guilty going. And fruitless too, for and after all my efforts the way ahead was still blocked.

Flustered and angry I struggled up the hill feeling flat and deflated. But things improved when I reached the top and took the Monarch's Way downhill, parallel to my original path. Reaching the junction at the valley bottom I estimated I'd enough time and the strength to go on to Old Winchester Hill. Then foolishly I took the wrong direction and after a mile had to retrace my steps, which meant wasted walking. Now I was feeling hungry, fatigued and frustrated.

For the first time I felt I was further from home than I'd thought and pressed for time with still some way to go to reach my second objective. So it was with a feeling of relief rather than a sense of achievement that I arrived at the site, now quite deserted. Then, after striding down the hill, I sat down on a log and ate some chocolate, but although it was bliss relaxing, I knew it would be fatal to sit for too long.

Clouds were now building up, dulling the bright blue of the sky and a cool breeze began to chill my skin. I was acutely aware it was half past two and still on unfamiliar territory. *How short these days are in the country in late November?* I thought to myself and cursed myself for having forgotten my mobile phone. I began finding it hard going but after trudging uphill for an hour I reached a village at three thirty. It was familiar but somehow knowing how far I still had to go made it seem worse, for my legs ached with weariness.

I crossed the main road and paused to take stock of my position. Dusk was fast approaching, and I now had to decide on my fastest way home. There was the long route along the main road or I could cut off to my left and follow the contours of the land on a sunken track I'd once used. Even in broad daylight I recalled disliking that path and didn't relish using it with evening coming on, aware that recent rain would make it muddy with long stretches of standing water. When I'd once used it the deeply hidden track, flanked by gnarled trees and misshapen bushes seemed to me have something *sinister* about it as if some ancient wrong had happened there. But taking it would save time and that was important.

I really had no choice and my misgivings about the route were soon more than justified. After twenty minutes' hard going it seemed as if all traces of humanity were far away and I'd intruded into a dark, primordial place. Foolish fears begin flitting through my mind as I pressed on finding it impossible to avoid sliding into potholes on the sunken track. I was now very tired and struggled along in the deep-set, silent and remote lane. It was quite dark in the rutted track hemmed in by rows of misshapen trees in the bare hedgerows and the only illumination was an occasional flash of moonlight gleaming for an instant on the stagnant, standing water.

Tiredness, isolation and an over-ripe imagination are powerful precursors of panicky thought and if you add to that my fear of animals, it's no wonder I thought of the Wendigo.

I first read about them in an Algernon Blackwood story and the thought of meeting one had haunted me ever since. Solitary and frightful to look at – like a gigantic horseshoe bat – they were said to dwell in unreachable parts of the great northern forests. The people of these Canadian wildernesses thought they carried with them a stench of death and decay and spoke of them only in daylight and not when the shadows lengthened. Some believed they exist to this day getting more powerful the longer they live, hunting by night and hating man.

If one sensed you, it would launch itself from the forest canopy, swoop down and clamp your body tight in its needle-sharp talons. And, when it landed, you'd be dragged beside it in great bounds until your bloodied feet were morphed into the shape of its cloven hooves. Once aloft again its headlong flight would force tears of blood from your eyes before its claws would open to drop you to earth, insane from the pain and shock. Such is a Wendigo, and such would be your fate if you met one at night. Surely no such awful creature could exist in the homely woods and meadows of Southern England? Or could it?

For some time stumbling along in the darkness I'd become aware of a shadowy form keeping pace behind the high bank on the opposite side of the track. I remember my heart pounding and my mouth becoming dry as I sneaked furtive sideways looks. *It must be a trick of the patchy moonlight*, I told myself for no figure ever appeared. But did it not move when I slogged and slithered along, sinking and disappearing when I stopped?

Then I found the empty car. Miles from anywhere and untidily parked near a group of trees where the track widened for a space. But what was it doing here, so abandoned? How had it got here, and where was the driver? And then a little way on I saw the broken shoe and then another some way away. I could hardly bear to look at them. I tried not to think of the bloody fate of the feet of those caught up by a Wendigo.

And then it happened. Struggling to avoid a deep wet rut I lost my balance on the muddy bank and fell, full-length into the water my foot trapped by a root and twisting my ankle as I slid sideways. Falling heavily is shocking even when you are fit and fresh but I was neither. And then came the icy grip of water penetrating my clothing, followed by a great stab of pain from my ankle, as I struggled to release my foot.

It seemed to go on and on but freed at last I collapsed onto the greasy mud bank, shivering and gasping with shock and pain. And as I slumped there, every sense sharp and tingling I remember a *noise* in the heavy silence – a hoarse sighing, overhead now, as if something monstrous and hungry with hatred, was searching for something. I strained my eyes but even when the cold light of the moon shone fitfully through the dead, empty branches all I saw was a dark, indistinct mass high up that could be anything. But I knew it was there as surely as I knew what it was.

Perhaps the owner of the car escaped and got away. I thought. *But I won't*. And part of me longed for the end to come swiftly, the manner of my passing more worrying than death itself. But it didn't come, and I never guessed why not.

After half an hour of utmost distress I began to wonder that, if the Wendigo hadn't decided what to do, perhaps it would let me struggle on to the end of the track. And that's exactly what I did. I then labored across a ploughed field to find a metalled road sloping gently running uphill to a line of woodland before descending into the valley where I was staying. And in open country with the moon now shining down from a cloudless sky and the track well behind me I could at last free my mind from fear. Somewhere along the way I found a branch that I could use as a crutch and with a huge feeling of relief I staggered along the road.

I saw the man coming towards me before he saw me and wondered why he kept looking up into the trees lining the road. As I approached him he stopped in surprise for it was a remote spot. Feeling faint I was close to collapse and sensing my distress he grasped my shoulders and urged me to sit down. I looked up at him and saw a heavily bearded, thickset man wearing what looked like a huge fur coat the hood of which was pulled up obscuring most of his face. There was a wildness about him and he had an odd smell – something deeply *natural* but somehow unsavoury.

He nodded sympathetically when I told him about the sunken track and my feelings about it.

'That cursed track was called Dead Man's Mile in ancient times,' he said, in a deep, thickly accented voice. 'Used to take condemned prisoners to be hanged after the assizes in Winchester.

No local would have gone that way on a dark night like this. Notice anything there when you hurt your ankle?'

And whether from the brandy he offered me in a hip flask or from relief I told him about the Wendigo.

'Hampshire isn't the Canadian backwoods is it?' he said, pocketing his flask. 'What would one be doing here. Paying us a flying visit?'

This was delivered without an ounce of humour, as if he really meant what he said.

'Not in *England*, no, no,' he murmured almost to himself, and them turning to me said urgently: 'But there *was* something bulky up in the tree that you thought was a Wendigo. Am I right?'

'Yes,' I said, struggling to get to my feet. Suddenly I just wanted to get away and I didn't want to speak to him anymore. But I was intrigued enough to ask what he was looking for when I first saw him.

'A young... creature,' he said. 'Damn thing got out and its mother will go mad if I don't find it before dawn. Maybe I'll go down Dead Man's Mile and see if it's there.'

'Good luck,' I said getting up as he turned to go. He briefly waved and I watched him hurrying down the road and then running like mad across the ploughed field leading to the awful track.

He vanished into the trees and I turned back along the road and so I never discovered what it was he was looking for or whether he found it. All I do know is that I could have sworn I heard a strange cry coming from the direction he'd taken and saw something like the shape of a huge bat rise above the trees for a brief moment before it disappeared into the gloom.

A trick of the moonlight on my over – stretched nerves? I thought, my heart beating. But I wasn't hanging around to find out the truth, whatever it was, so I'll never know.

Of one thing I'm certain and that is that I'll never ever go down that track again. And if you were alone as I was in that cursed lane on that dark night you'd *know* that there are things dwelling in such places which are best avoided. Real but indescribable things like the horrors known to the native people when the shadows gather in the great forests of the north.

But nameless in England, for does not *naming* them give them a kind of *reality* that we prefer to believe doesn't exist. Even though we fear it does when the wind whistles round our chimneys and we lie like frightened children clutching the sheets in the dead of night.

PASSING THOUGHTS

ike most people's lives mine consisted of two things: me and the things that happened to me. And, although I accept they influenced each other, coming from Barnsley I've always called a spade a bloody shovel, and tended to interpret the things I had to deal with in life in the same way. And it wasn't easy – there were always people and problems getting in the way of me doing things properly, the way I liked them, and helping me live a decent life, not some soft existence like life for southerners when there's some hard graft to do. But insurance assessors like me never let obstacles like that interfere with doing my duty.

After I passed (I prefer "died") I was asked to think about what I'd like to do to move on spiritually. Initially I thought of "death watch" because I felt I might meet like spirits who were averse to funereal frivolity. Some hopes! I admit my life inclined towards the frugal and practical rather than the flippant and shallow but as a raw spirit the rank hypocrisy shown at my funeral ceremony and the pleasure just *pouring* from my family was unforgivable. I mentioned this at my review and a Senior Soul agreed I should attend these gatherings to see what I might learn about my own life. I don't know why – I'd still live it just the same.

I like to be formally dressed at funerals but no one notices. How could they? And I like a good cry as much as anyone, so I look for signs of genuine grief. I don't mean drunken Celtic wailing but the real thing although it's so rare. Most of those "paying their respects" are only there for the food, the fashion or the gossip. All three if their luck's in.

I much prefer a dismal, rain-swept, grave-side ceremony to a cremation although I'd always liked the gush of emotion that came with the swish of the curtains covering the coffin. It's seen as too harrowing for mourners to have to face the *finality* of death and so they don't do it now. That's a shame because I believe funerals are places of pain and grief and not some "celebration of the life of the departed" with everyone in bright clothes, "reaching out" to all and sundry. Man born to misery can surely go out the same way without a lot of fancy dressing up and everyone *grappling* with each other.

Of course, I can't interfere with the ceremony or the living congregation, but I can still breathe a bit of solemnity into the proceedings by *wafting* the odd gust of chill air over the coughers or glare at some loathsome tot. If the brat is not long out of the womb it'll recognise a like-spirit and put in some hearty wailing.

There's a rumour that I'm being moved to do a stint in the House of Commons, patrolling a few of the lesser used passageways where the wages of sin subsidise sudden heart attacks from older Members liaising with their young support staff. It sounds rather undignified, but it could it lead to an international career – perhaps even an exchange with a stint in the sacred White House itself. Much more respectable than the sordid British Parliament to be in a venerable place like the Oval Office! The epitome of High Office and restrained impeccable conduct.

There was a lot of nudging among jealous souls when I mentioned it and someone sniggered "Zippergate Zone". I guess it's likely to be some comment about a dress code which I'll have to find out about and prepare for with some care.

THE TINDER AND THE SPARK

I dreamed I was in the retreat where I used to go to forget the noise and news of modern life. For the most part it was a haven of calm and quiet, especially for those like me who stayed overnight. For then the day visitors had gone, taking with them their noisy discussion of the works of the visionary who was the inspiration behind the place.

If you stayed you had a clean, uncluttered room, no television or alcohol and as much or as little companionship as you wanted. And you could wander through the pleasant local Hampshire countryside and for meals there was always a table where, if you wished, you could sit alone. I preferred eating with others which I sometimes regretted, for gentle doctrines can attract adherents less interested in searching for their understanding than proclaiming half-baked interpretations of what they think they mean. When I'd had enough of this I usually went to the library where I could be sure of being alone.

It was a spacious, attractive room, heavily carpeted and furnished with armchairs as well as a desk for those who wished to write. I never saw it used, for much of the founder's works were available on other media, and most visitors preferred to watch and listen rather than read. To be fair to them, the founder wrote copiously without expressing his views briefly and clearly and that didn't make for easy reading.

His was a unique approach to the great personal issues of birth, life and death which he expressed in a continuous kind of stream of consciousness writing which I found irritating and exhausting to follow. And yet he was acclaimed internationally for his insight and spiritual acuity and I often felt isolated and out of sympathy with those I met there for their uncritical acceptance of his words. For the most part they were sensitive, intelligent people and I felt envious of their genuine commitment and wondered what it was I'd missed.

But the retreat was a truly great achievement and worked well to realise the founder's vision. Or so I thought.

The setting for my dream was the library where I was sitting alone after dinner with the soft table lamps casting a warm glow over the comfortable room. It was very quiet and peaceful and I was dozing for I'd walked many miles that day. And then I noticed a small figure sitting in the shadows before the empty fireplace. I nodded to him and he smiled.

'You are often here, I think,' he said, in the precise but accented tones of an educated Indian.

'I find it calming and I love being surrounded by books.'

'But you do not read them,' he said, as if he'd watched me over a long period.

'I come here to think,' I said, defensively, for what he said was true.

'Very wise,' he said. 'There's not much here worth the effort of reading.'

'Oh, I don't know,' I protested. 'People I respect seem to find things in the works here that elude me. But I'm rather impatient and I probably miss what others find who search more diligently.'

'It is a quality we share, my friend,' he said. 'But you also possess another *essence* that permits us to talk like this.'

'I wonder what that might be?'

'It doesn't have a name it is excessively rare.'

'Can you describe it?' I said, trying to look serious.

'You'll find you occasionally combine disparate parts of existence, like the past and the future, the living and the dead, the conscious and the dream-world,' he said. 'And that is very unusual in a human.'

'I've never been considered particularly clever.'

'Ah, you mean you didn't do well enough at *exams*. The western curse, finding such fertile ground to breed in India, of acquiring facts and legitimising your possession of them through "objective" testing.'

'I suppose so,' I said, half hoping he'd leave me alone and chatter on like this to someone else.

'*My* insight,' he said. 'Also suggests that you have *curiosity*.'

'Well, I like to know about all sorts of things, and watch to see how situations turn out because I'm often surprised by unforeseen outcomes.'

'I wonder if you will like my surprise,' he said.

'Which is?'

'By the side of this very comfortable armchair,' he said tapping something metallic, 'I have a can of petrol.'

'Now you're making me very curious,' I said. *And very alarmed,* I thought.

'I think you'd agree with me' he said. 'That most of the volumes here are indulgently conceived and too inaccessibly wordy to be easily assimilable and consequentially quite properly unread. Time to get rid of them. What do you say?'

'If you mean you intend to set them alight I think it's terribly wrong to burn books. It always leads to much greater desecration of things like human rights, freedom of speech and civil liberties.'

'Words, words, words,' he said getting up. 'Promise me you'll read tonight what I suggest.'

'Very well,' I said.

'There's a book on that shelf, called "Russian Writers",' he said, pointing. 'And in it you'll learn what Gogol did to the second and third manuscripts of his work, *'Dead Souls'*. And when you wake up, remember what you've read.'

Lifting the can with an effort he nodded, walked to the door and closed it quietly, leaving me alone. Unsettled I paced around the room and then went to the shelf and picked out the book he'd indicated.

Still dreaming, I read that Nikolai Gogol wrote part one of *Dead Souls* intending it to be the first volume of a great revelation to mankind, equivalent to Dante's *Hell*, with parts two and three corresponding to Purgatory and Heaven. His aim was to reveal to Russia the righteous way of living and to "effect moral improvement through his art". But later he felt not only was his talent insufficient but the work itself was ungodly. And so he burned the manuscripts, took to his bed and died nine days later of starvation.

Next in my dream I was at reception in the retreat talking to Erich who was on duty that night.

'I've been in the library,' I said 'And I was talking to a man who had a can of petrol. I think he wanted to set fire to the books.'

'What was he like?'

'Small and slightly built, Asian features, spoke English very quickly with an Indian accent.'

'Did he say anything?' said Erich.

'He said I was unusual and curious.'

'Did he say anything about the books in there?'

'He said they were unintelligible. Just an ego at work writing random thoughts without restraint.'

'Are you sure that's what he said?'

'The gist of it. So why is he here if he thinks like that?'

'Who can tell?' said Erich. 'It sounds to me like the man who wrote them, and he died years ago'

'I never met him,' I said, weakly.

'Perhaps after he died, he found out the truth of what he'd written.'

'Would he have really burned the library down?'

'Someone did years ago. Didn't you know? Didn't you know? Didn't you know?'

And then another voice shouted 'Wake up, wake up, wake up!' and I was home in bed and my wife was telling me to get up.

★ ★ ★

My heart was pounding for the dream had been so detailed and vivid that there was only one thing I could do. I drove for hours to the retreat where I hadn't been for many years and found it still there but with a new building in place of the library I knew. Inside I found that the man on reception was Androv, the new director. I introduced myself and spoke of my many visits to the retreat.

'I see the old library's gone,' I said.

'There was a fire some years back,' he said.

'Do they know what caused it?'

'Not really, but there was talk of arson.'

'Why on earth would someone want burn it down?' I said 'And what made them think it was deliberate?'

'It was before my time,' he said. 'But Danilo, one of the staff locking up said he heard voices in the library on the night it happened. But who they were was a mystery because all the guests had gone to bed.'

'How odd.'

'What was even stranger was later when he passed the library after leaving the keys in reception he glanced in and saw a large book lying open on the table by the chair.'

'Did he look at it?' I asked, my heart beginning to race.

'More than that I understand Danilov who was Ukrainian took it back to his room to check on something. He moved on some time ago – as you know we have staff from all over the world.'

'Actually I know what it was,' I blurted out. "*Great Russian Writers*", and it was open in the library to an entry about Gogol!'

'I don't understand,' he said giving me a quick glance, quietly reaching for the phone.

'Nor do I,' I replied. 'But believe me, I really wish I did!'

I looked so distressed that Androv, after getting a colleague to take over reception, took me to a secluded part of the garden and we talked about my experience.

'Routine and familiar things comfort us and help persuade us our lives are rooted in what we call "reality",' he said. 'But we forget that for a third of that time we are unconscious and asleep, and we naturally assume that periods awake and asleep are separate states. But that's not quite true.'

'So how can the dream-time conversation I had between myself and a dead person be heard by a living man like Danilov?' I said, 'He even found physical evidence of the book I dreamed I was reading? It's truly frightening. '

'What is it you fear most?'

'That in not liking the founder's writings I was partly to blame for the burning down of his library,' I said.

'So you fear that a *dream-time* conversation with him led to the *actual* burning down of the library?'

'Yes,' I said. 'Was I the spark that ignited the tinder in him causing him to destroy his work?'

'There's not a shred of evidence about that,' said Androv. 'And an open verdict was recorded about the fire.'

'If so why do I feel guilt over something of which I had no conscious control?'

'Would it help if I told you that no fewer than ten other people have come to me with the same story and concerns?' he said.

'Immeasurably,' I said.

'Sometimes for unknown reasons these things just happen,'

he said. 'So much of life is beyond our senses or our minds' grasp. Don't worry it's unlikely to happen again.'

'If it's just a one off unexplained event I can relax now,' I said. 'If it had been an on-going gift I wouldn't want it, because I wouldn't know how to use it to help others.'

And so I left the retreat where I'd spent many happy hours without a backward glance. And nothing remotely like it ever happened again.

★ ★ ★

It was just as well I didn't hear Androv talking to someone later that night.

'Why do you go on doing it?' he said. 'You know the fire was an accident but oh no, you just go on winding them up because of what they thought about your work. It's just mischief making, and I'm going to get some mature spirits together and we're going to dream-team you away to a different place now you're dead. And we'll make sure you lose that tired old can of petrol you keep wandering around with – it's not as if there was anything in it in the first place!'

SECOND-HAND SPIRIT

H arley Street surgeons aren't expected to leap from their beds in the early hours to stem some toddler's nosebleed and nor should Senior Spiritual Consultants have to waste time using state of the art equipment in so-called haunted gimcrack tourist traps like the "Treasure Trove of Terror". But Hilda, my director told me to go there at once and I'd hardly stepped off the plane from Haiti where I'd been representing the bureau at the Voodoo Queen Memorial Meet in Haiti.

'Can't some *novice* go?' I asked. 'It's only a "bedspring" job. That's our term for reports of "ethereal vibrations" in the early hours which often turn out to be neighbours testing mattresses.

'It's a direct request from our president,' she said, no doubt imagining that rigid with terror, I'd spring to attention. 'And it came to him from Lord Flack who owns a lot of seaside novelty shops, bingo parlours and amusement arcades.'

'Refined connections, then,' I said.

Hilda gave me one of her quick glances to show she wasn't in the mood for levity.

'His Lordship,' she said. 'Is very *thick* with the Lord Lieutenant and the wives play bridge with our president's missus and the chief constable's intern when she's not on traffic duty. It's a purple directive: "Send best pronto".'

'I know how these things go,' I said wearily. 'I've just staggered into the empty office to check my mail and next thing I find I'm your "best pronto".'

'Lucky for some,' said Hilda. 'Especially for you after getting the hot-ticket Haitian jolly that everybody else was after.'

'OK, *OK*,' I said 'Don't get on your broomstick. Just tell me what you want me to do!'

'Apparently in His Lordship's empire one hot little earner is or rather *was,* a novelty shop in Devon, specialising in horror rubbish for kids of all ages,' she said. 'It's in some dump called Lympton and goes by the name of the "Treasure Trove of Terror".'

'Blood curdling!'

'Lympton,' she said, glaring at me. 'As you will find out from a diligent scrutiny of its public relations literature, "Nestles snugly behind high cliffs".'

'And after a red eye flight it's me who should be following its lead and in bed asleep,' I said, my lighthearted manner concealing deep dismay.

'You can be so *annoying,* Eugene,' she said. 'Do you know that?'

'Yes, but I'm totally at your disposal now,' I said, snapping smartly out of "winsome" into "action mode".

'The shop in question was built right up against these cliffs, and there's a passage from it leading straight into the rockface.'

'Artificial or natural, old or recent?' I said, the news igniting a tiny spark of interest.

'Probably artificial, but old,' Hilda said. '*Very* old, judging from the reports of a local geologist.'

'Why would a geologist, local or otherwise be interested in a passage like that?'

'She didn't know what she was doing there either,' said Hilda. Some halfwit at Flack's Media Centre, came up with the bright idea that "modern moms" might send their tiny treasures on an escorted trip along the passage called "Happy Halloween Hauntings Trip". But the tots all screamed with terror during the experience and suffered from nightmares afterwards. So it was obvious that a geologist might help explain what happened.'

'What sort of experiences and dreams?'

'Unseen hands touching them, whisperings and icy draughts, as far as I can make out from the president.'

'Kids get scared,' he said. 'Isn't that the whole point of the exercise?'

'Not so intensely and not so *consistently* afterwards.'

'Did the geologist come up with anything?'

'She produced this huge report which in essence said the passage was cold, damp and draughty,' Hilda said. 'And that might have caused the problem.'

'The longer I live...' I said. 'But seriously, I suppose the little shop of horrors was closed down?'

'Yes, largely owing to the exertions of the local council's Inclusive Outreach Committee,' said Hilda. 'Who, oddly enough, seem to hate Tory peers. The owner of the shop is just such a person – did I tell you that?'

'Yes, you did. And also that his wife likes bridge and probably opens two clubs with less than ten points.'

'Eugene dear, you're sounding tired,' said Hilda. 'Dear-heart, just go down there and see what's going on will you? You can pick up the keys of the place from the local estate agent. You'll also probably meet some kind of caretaker who might be lurking around the area doing nothing, like you were in Haiti.'

'Hilda, my Directrice, I'll give it my best shot,' I said. 'And I'll be back before you can say "abracadabra".'

'I'll practice it while you're gone,' she said, grinning. *Not a bad sort old Hilda,* I'd always thought.

★ ★ ★

After packing the gear in the Land Rover, I left the next day and around five o'clock picked up the keys from Giles Harbin, the local estate agent.

'You'll probably need them to get in,' he said. 'Some old chap *loiters* around there but nobody seems to know what he does or who he belongs to. I keep well away from the whole thing, and I advise you to do the same.'

I got to the empty shop as dusk was falling making it seem even more unwelcoming than I imagine it was in the day. With a deep sigh of resignation, I opened the front door and after inhaling an invigorating chestful of dusty, stale air from within I pushed past the usual tourist junk of Halloween skeletons, inflatable pumpkins and child-friendly facemasks.

Now for all my engaging frivolity I'm in the occult investigation business for the very good reason that I'm a genuine Spirit Sensitive and this place for all its cheap gimcrackery was setting off a few alarm bells in my head. Exactly why was hard to pin down, but even for an old pro like me it was punching above its weight in the spiritual league.

Suddenly a light came on and a man appeared from a door behind the counter.

'You made me jump,' I said, the nerves already on high alert.

'My dear Sir, do forgive me,' he said, in a precise, cultured voice. 'I live in another part of this same building and heard a noise.'

'I'm so sorry to disturb you,' I said 'But I was given to understand that the shop was empty. The agent gave me the key to get in.'

While I was speaking I looked him over for I've found over the years that you can learn a lot from resident loonies caretaking haunted houses and he looked like a prime specimen. He was a whispy, sallow, thin-faced chap wearing an egg-stained, old -boys tie of some fatuous public school and an ancient tweed jacket with leather elbow patches. When I introduced myself he nodded whilst weaving about as if reluctant to make contact and his handshake was limp, bony and brief.

'I'm Miles Mildmay,' he said. 'Caretaker and odd job man.'

'And I'm here because of the problems experienced by children in the passage. Can you help me?'

'Problem?' he said vaguely. 'Children? Sally Marsden's girl looks after all that side of things... I just tidy up and things like that. I thought we'd finished showing them round.'

'Who?'

'The children, of course,' he said, irritably. 'Didn't they tell you?'

'Tell me what?'

'That you won't find them here, now,' he muttered. 'Those who you're looking for... rather late in the day. I'm sorry I'm afraid I get rather muddled these days.'

'Are you running the shop alone, Sir?' I asked the old fool.

'Just fillin' in, fillin' in,' he almost whispered.

'Can you show me the passage?'

'Can't *show* you,' he said. 'No, no that wouldn't do, at all.'

'Can you tell me *anything* about the passage, Mr Mildmay?'

'Mrs Marsden's your route to that,' he said. 'Haven't been down that passage for years. Don't know what I'd find there if I did. Best left alone.'

I felt I was losing my grip on reality, but he seemed harmless enough and I persevered.

'If I wanted to speak to her where could I find her?'

'She'll be out soon,' I expect, he said looking at the clock on the wall.

'Where from?'

'About now,' he said, pointing to an ancient oak door at the rear of the shop.

It was then I recalled that the shop was built against a cliff and what I'd taken to be the back wall was in fact the rock face. Doubtless the old doorway guarded the entrance to the "haunted cave" deep inside the cliff and there I'd find a narrow, descending passage. And *that* was what I'd come to investigate. But I was getting nowhere and, while I was wondering what to do, I heard a knock on the front door. Outside stood a kindly looking but anxious middle-aged lady.

'Mr Harbin the estate agent asked me to call by on my way home, Sir,' she said. 'Hello Mr Mildmay,' she said, seeing him and he smiled jerking around like a marionette doll. 'Can I help you with anything?' she continued.

'Yes, please,' I said, looking back into the dim interior. 'Perhaps if I come out?'

She nodded and after stepping outside and quietly closing the door I introduced myself to her and she said she was Joan Marsden.

'I'm here to help find out what it was that frightened the children,' I said. 'You do know what I'm referring to?'

'Oh yes, Sir,' she said, with a worried look. 'I do hope you can throw some light on it, if only for poor old Mr Mildmay's sake. He's the one in charge of the place.'

'Can you give me some background to the use of the passage?'

'Well, Sir,' she said. 'Before Lord Flack took over, the door to the passage was always locked, but then young Mr Giles at Gilbrook and Hardin took instructions about opening it up to take the kiddies round on a spooky little trip. And they asked me to take them round.'

'Did you know about the passage?'

'We local girls heard about it,' she said. 'It was said to be haunted, but none of us ever went there. Couldn't if we wanted to – it was always locked up.'

'What happened then.'

These nice young ladies came down from Lord Flack's London Office and put a few little harmless scary objects in the passage and lit them up from behind. The kids loved it.'

'It all sounds quite harmless,' I said. 'So, what do you think caused the nightmares?'

'I don't know, Sir,' she said. 'But it seems it all started when I had to go and look after my sister's boy. Only Mr Mildmay was around, and I suppose he just let the kids go in on their own with the parents. None of the grown-ups had any problems.'

'What do you know about him?' I asked.

'It was his grandson who ran the shop before Lord Flack bought it,' she said. 'He comes from an aristocratic family who go way back in these parts, but not too clever now poor old gentleman.'

'Can you show me the passage?'

'I'm sorry, Sir, but I must be getting home,' she said, hurriedly. 'It's just a passage through the rock with a sort of cave at the end, not very long. But you'll need to light the candles in the wall niches, and I was told you *must* wear gloves when you're inside. Always, but I don't know why. And that's what we tell everyone who goes in there.'

'Thank you, Mrs Marsden,' I said. 'In our experience what people feel is the supernatural often turns out to have quite a mundane explanation.'

'I dare say you're right, Sir,' she said.

'If you don't mind Mr Mildmay I'll just look inside the passage,' I shouted across to him. 'And I'll light the candles in the niches.' He smiled vaguely at me from the other side of the shop and then resumed dosing in a chair behind the counter.

The shadows of a late September day were already moving along the walls and darkening the corners of the room when I returned to the shop having inspected the passage and lighted the candles. It was about thirty yards long and broadened out into a small cave about fifteen feet square and perhaps eight feet high. The passage had been hewn out of the limestone using basic hand-tools and in the light of my torch the walls glistened with moisture highlighting the intricate patterns of seashells impressed into the soft rock. In the cave was a raised area against one wall like a seat or perhaps a low altar, but I couldn't yet detect anything other than a cold, humid damp smell just like many other underground places I'd explored.

Returning to the shop I glanced across at the old boy, now gently snoring, and began lugging the equipment from the Landrover to the passage. There were high resolution cameras, temperature recorders, speech detectors and infra-red and ultra-violet lamps. All the paraphernalia of the modern ghost hunter. Moving it into the cave took my mind off the things and when everything was finally set up, I told Mildmay I was ready to begin.

'One thing before I leave it to you,' he said. 'It might get cold in there, but you can briefly remove your gloves when you have to adjust your equipment, whatever you heard to the contrary.'

'Thanks for the advice,' I said. 'Rest assured I can't manage delicate equipment with gloves on even if I start out by wearing them.'

'Well done, my boy,' he said, smiling for the first time.

★ ★ ★

Mildmay then disappeared so I pulled on the gloves left on a table in the shop, opened the heavy oak door and entered the dark world of the passageway beyond.

If there's anything more effective for undermining your feeling of security than being alone in a dark, silent cave after the busy world of light I don't know what it is. In spite of all my years of doing it I'd never lost the dryness in my throat, the tightness in the chest and the elevated heartbeat that always comes in such a place and that's why we usually work with a partner. But on this job, of course, I was alone.

With all my equipment primed and ready to operate I sat on a small collapsible stool and waited in the deep silence. Waiting was always the worst part! Nothing happened for about an hour, and then the temperature of the cave fell, almost imperceptibly at first, and then more rapidly. Soon I could see my breath in the light of the lamps and I pulled my anorak more tightly around my shoulders. This change was not unusual, but it's always unnerving when you're alone.

And then, as the temperature plummeted still further my sensitive equipment began to flicker and fail. Dark shadows leapt forward in place of the lamp light and I strained to hear the slightest noise. But all was silent as I checked my equipment and, needing to adjust a few delicate knobs, slipped off my gloves. Instantly I felt a small cool hand grasp mine and squeeze it – just like a gentle caress and only for a moment. *How odd to feel such a gesture of human reassurance in the circumstances* I thought. But there was no time to look at what had grasped my hand, if indeed it was other than in my imagination. Then the temperature began to rise, my equipment started working and light flooded back into the cave.

I felt strangely drained and shivery as if he had a cold coming on and tried to restrain my urgent need to be outside. Thinking that Mildmay might be waiting, I walked along the passage into the shop and he looked up as I approached him.

'See anything?' he said, and I shook my head. '*Feel* anything?' he said, looking at my gloved hands.

'Well actually it seemed as if someone held my hand,' I said. 'I only slipped off my gloves for a second and it happened then.'

'Let's take a look at your hand, my boy,' he said, suddenly very tense.

I pulled off the gloves and looked at my hands and my heart missed a beat. The right hand was delicate, small and well-shaped. Rather pretty but the only thing wrong was that it wasn't mine. You must believe me it wasn't *mine*. It just wasn't!

'Thank God!' he said. 'I've got mine back – look.'

He showed me his hands both mottled and marked with age but indisputably a pair.

'I must go, I must go!' he cried.

'Don't,' I shouted, but he ran through the door into his room and disappeared into the shadows. In a moment I was almost alone. Almost.

For a soft, insistent voice from the passage was saying 'Coming, coming,' as if calling me back and I looked at my new hand and knew it was already too late. Whatever was in there wasn't going to let me go, and I'd no idea what it was or what it wanted. All I knew was that I dreaded being drawn against my will towards that awful summons.

★ ★ ★

It should have ended there, and it nearly did. But I had one chance and one alone. I phoned Hilda.

'What do you want?' she said. 'I'm just going home?'

'"SST",' I said, my ears picking up the sound of soft footsteps from the passage behind the open oak door.

When practitioners face desperate situations, some professional organisations have code words or procedures for them to use in extreme peril. The police have one to which all officers must respond when it's activated. In the bureau "Sierra Sierra Tango", stands for "Serious Spiritual Threat" and is only used in the most desperate circumstances.

Can you picture the scene? A dim, dark evening in a dank, dismal shop with some unknown creature beckoning to you and the wrist of your right arm terminating in an alien hand. I'd like to say I uttered something amusing but there was no time.

'I have your co-ordinates,' Hilda said, calmly. 'Hold on, do nothing and keep your fears under control.'

But was the nearest help nearer than the nearby threat? Bearing that in mind while keeping calm was like telling someone in the grip of a grizzly to relax and think positively.

The footsteps in the passage were coming nearer and then in the flickering light of the candles in the passage, a figure appeared.

'Mrs Marsden!' I croaked.

'Hello my dear,' she laughed. 'I guess I can call you that for we're going to be together for a long time, my darling. First a handshake to seal the bargain and then a kiss of welcome.' She held out her arms and I felt the hand pulling me towards her.

All I remember then was a *dullish* flash and a dark shape coming between us.

'So this is what you've been up to, Julia,' said Hilda, her form at first wavery and indistinct and then firmer, showing her astonishing ability to astral project. 'After you left the Portsmouth Poltergeist Ring penniless and then the Spectral Scrying Circle in Southampton with all the profits you went to ground here. This tired old poltergeist playground! I thought its power had dissipated years ago.'

'Just a bit of harmless fright phobia for a few kids, Hilda,' said Mrs Marsden. 'Had to keep my hand in.'

'Better to have kept it to yourself, Julia,' said Hilda. 'And you can give my Senior Investigator his back and keep yours to yourself. Don't dare use that trick again as bait to get some innocent like my poor boy into your clutches. Like you did to poor old Mildmay. But he wasn't much use to you was he? So you needed someone else to do your dirty work.'

'What now, Hilda?' said Mrs Marsden, biting her lip.

'You'll come back with me and face the music with my chairman for a start,' said Hilda. 'But make sure you've released Mildmay for good and get out of the body of that poor woman. I'll give you a temporary astral body to come with me and you may get your proper one back if you behave yourself.'

Joan Marsden snarled but sank to the ground and then a peaceful look came over her face as a scruffy tomcat minus one ear appeared from nowhere. I burst into laughter and the cat looked at me with infinite disgust. That was followed by another wave of relieved hilarity as the form of Hilda picked it up and then their forms wavered, faded and then disappeared.

'Thanks… Hilda,' I said lamely to thin air, and then rang the office.

'I thought I told you I was going home,' she said, when she took my call. 'And you can stay there and sort out the mess you've made of a simple poltergeist job and get back here on Monday. I've got more important things for you to do than waste your time at the seaside and you only just returned from holiday in Haiti! I must be mad, but I'm glad you're back.'

She comes over to some as harsh, but to my way of thinking when it matters she never lets you down, doesn't Hilda. One of the very, very best, bless her!

THE AGE OF ANXIETY

'Oh God,' Angus cried out, staring in horror at the stray hairs in his hairbrush. 'I'll soon be as bald as a coot.' Carefully combing back the thick hair from his forehead he first peered closely at his hairline, his pulses racing, and then used the wall mirror to get a view of the crown of his head. He stared aghast at the tiny patch of scalp showing pink at the end of his parting. So it had come at last. The inexorable start and the end of days. The moment he had dreaded since childhood thirty years before.

Ageing was so hard to bear when he spent so much time and money in keeping fit and healthy. He was regular in his sessions at the gym and subscribed and read publications devoted to men's health, and even some to women's wellbeing. Many women might have benefitted from his knowledge of HRT or the best way of assisting in a birth on the back seat of a taxi going to the hospital.

He cycled at speed to his office in Bloomsbury every day where he conducted his actuarial business with precision and competence. He ate and drank sensibly, and his sexual life was regular if rather dull. So far so good. But lurking beneath the well regulated exterior was a festering, un-lanced boil of sheer terror at the thought of getting old.

The utter *obscenity* of sagging flesh and wrinkled skin and then the callouses, corns, chilblains, incontinence, heart disease, cancer and dementia. And all the undignified appurtenances needed to keep going even after nature had set the bar too high for an unaided human. Glasses, dentures, hearing aids, hernia supports – even surgical boots. Props to buy a few years more to sustain the crumbling ruin of a body racked with pain and festooned with the scars of a hundred surgical interventions. And to cap it all going bald.

He gave a great sigh and went down to breakfast where he found Tanya, his beautiful Russian wife, reading a fashion magazine and smoking at the table. Hastily opening a window he said casually, 'I think I'm losing my hair.'

'In my country is sign of virility,' she murmured, automatically turning a page of her magazine.

'Well not in Penge, it's not!' he shouted, wondering for the umpteenth time how he'd ended up with a mail order bride as stupid as her. 'Look at this!' he screamed, pulling back his hair to show the unblemished hairline, trembling with irritation and anxiety.

Tanya looked briefly at the follicular display and with a loud sigh returned to her article.

Angus, after his unusual display of emotion sank into a chair exhausted.

'You just don't know how important this is to me, do you?' he groaned head in his hands. 'Oh God I just can't bear it.'

He was on the verge of hysteria and that was rare enough to worry Tanya. She was very fond of the well-off, hard-working but obsessive little Scotsman and wanted to help, even though she didn't understand what all the fuss was about. Then she had an idea.

When she'd had problems with her hair she'd found it useful to see Madame Tissot, a Spiritual Guide, a luminary located in Sidcup. From her ministrations Tanya emerged focused, energised and eighty pounds poorer. She hadn't told her husband about the sessions and had to be careful about suggesting he visit Madame.

'Husband,' she said. 'Have heard of Spiritual Health Consultant, very good, help people who worry about health. I have address. Learn truth then prepare for worst – or make best of it.'

Madame Tissot, in her private life Mrs Maureen Wilkins, was a large, middle-aged woman dressed in a colourful array of flowing silk garments. Angus, who'd been expecting some urbane Harley Street quack was surprised at the address and her appearance and felt rather foolish as he explained why he was there. He would have felt less concerned if he'd know how innocuous his request was in the strange world of the occultist.

After some palm reading, crystal gazing and tarot card readings Madame delivered her verdict.

'Not only will you retain your hair for the rest of your life but you will continue with good health until you die,' she said. 'That will be a hundred pounds, please.'

Thrilled by her words Angus willingly parted with the money and rose to leave. As they shook hands Madame looked hard at him for a moment and then made as if to speak. But she must have thought better of it for she ushered him out in silence.

★ ★ ★

'They get younger all the time,' said the paramedic to her as they lifted Angus's lifeless body into the ambulance. 'I mean, look at this bloke. Steps out your door, massive heart attack, dead before he reaches the ground. Bloody tragic.'

Madam Tissot looked down, without shock or surprise, at the body now covered up in the ambulance before they closed the doors. 'Yes,' she said quietly. 'And he had so much to look forward to!'

TOEING THE LINE

J ack and I always shared a great interest in the Georgian British Navy, especially around the time of Nelson and many people will have an image of the great "line of battle" ships that fought at Trafalgar. But although we admired these great vessels, they never possessed the swashbuckling appeal for us of what were known as the "eyes and ears" of the fleet – the free-roving frigates with bold career captains and their hair-raising adventures. And the seamen who lived and fought in these ships were no less extraordinary than their officers.

For a brief period, only a hundred years or so, a way of life existed in which wooden ships of war were commanded by professional sailors, often at sea since they were ten years old. It was they who had to man and provision their ships and then train and lead a crew, many of whom were pressed landsmen. These men had to learn to handle ropes and sails in all winds and weathers, man guns and board ships to kill or subdue foreign seamen who they were told were their enemies. Without these men, many dragged unwillingly from their inland lives and subject to brutal punishments, the greatest empire the world had ever seen would never have been created or sustained. For it was these legendary "hearts of oak" who were the forerunners of those who made the Royal Navy the global power it became.

The ships built for war in which they sailed were also their home for years and although understandably resentful at their recruitment the life many of the landsmen endured was scarcely less harsh than life afloat. Instead of ceaseless unpaid, toil on the land for their masters and being village bound for much of their lives, joining the navy might have some compensations. Imagine such men setting foot on a foreign shore for the first time rather than tramping the same old fields year after year, and even the terror of wild northern weather being offset by balmy nights in the tropics. Receiving regular food and rudimentary medical treatment when sick as well as wounded would be a great improvement on their life on land. Would they have had the opportunity for lifelong fellowship with others facing the same hardships, or acquired undreamt-of skills where none existed before? Or had a share, however small, of prize money?

But Jack's interest went further than mine and he began creating beautiful replicas of the Georgian frigates. Ever the perfectionist he began his ship-building career "learning the ropes" on repetitive tasks like making and laying deck planking. But, as his hands became more adept, he found his involvement in the period moving to another level – towards a deep feeling of *fellowship* to the unknown craftsmen who designed and built these ships. And often, when worn out after a long day's work Jack told me he could almost sense the presence of craftsmen who created ships to withstand the worst the seas could throw against them and still be able to give and receive savage punishment against skilled opponents. Where, he wondered, did this knowledge and those skills come from?

In England, France and Spain the knowledge and skills must have originated from medieval masters who created wooden masterpieces like the Great Octagonal Lantern in Ely Cathedral, Notre Dame or the massive eight-hundred-year-old hammer-beam roof of Westminster Hall. And much of this knowledge and skill would have gradually permeated down to local craftsmen throughout the land.

Jack's devotion to his craft led to an interest that became a passion deepening his insight into what guided his predecessors in their design and building of these great war machines. Then he took a false step. He began to *innovate* and make small adjustments to the late eighteenth-century vessels he was re-creating. And increasingly the models he built – and now they were getting bigger – incorporated elements never part of a real ship that lifted to a tide or weathered a gale. But although he felt he could change details he always remained faithful to square-rigged, wooden period ships always striving to improve his craftmanship.

And then came the reckoning. Late one night, toiling alone in his workshop connecting some ratlines to the shrouds on a frigate's mainmast he heard a respectful cough. Swinging round in his chair, his heart beating wildly, he perceived a large man standing awkwardly behind him, twisting a woollen hat in his hands. Burly, hirsute and tanned wearing a long greasy pigtail he was dressed in dirty, ill-fitting clothes and smelled oddly pungent.

'Who are you?' Jack cried out, reaching for a small Japanese saw before realising its offensive limitations.

'Jem Shrubsole, late Masters Mate, Sir,' said the man, knuckling his forehead in a gesture known as "making his obedience". 'Come bearing a message.'

'Message?'

'The gentlemen of the Portsmouth dockyard have been taking a keen interest in your work, Sir,' said Jem. 'And very pleased with it they've been – and the Board of Admiralty too, from what I've heard. Even though it's a dry-dock building some do say, beggin' yore pardon, Sir.'

'I'm delighted they like my work,' said Jack, modestly.

'Truth to tell, Sir,' said Jem, awkwardly, 'I'm charged to say: "No more".'

'No more of what?'

'Fantastical notions, departures from what's natural,' Jem said. 'Look at that fancy rigging of yours – wouldn't hold up for a brace in a smart sou-wester without a wealth of puddening needed. If you was up that mast and in a real, fresh north easterly you'd soon see where my argument's leading.'

'Perhaps I've *deviated* a touch on the original design using my own bracing but what about my other improvements,' said Jack. 'Slight hull modifications with considerable drag-reduction coefficients stemming from my computer-generated designs?'

'Never you mind that old box of tricks,' said Jem, darkly. 'My advice, Sir, is to steer a course back to the old ways, or else.'

'Or else what?'

'Or, beggin' your pardon, Sir,' said Jem. 'I'm to come back with another sort of message and one that's more *sparse* on words than this one. A belayin' pin can speak wondrous clear in the right hands.'

And with that he made his obedience and disappeared.

★ ★ ★

Unfortunately that all came at a bad time for Jack who was about to have surgery on his jaw. But what concerned him more than the threat of violence was the feeling that he'd let down his mentors. *Perhaps I have been rather too experimental,* he thought…

I saw him in his hospital bed shortly afterwards feeling sore and made more miserable by his feeling that he'd betrayed those whose work he so admired.

'I wish I could get word to them,' he said. 'I'll gladly do what they want.'

'Can I help?' I said, trying to forget I was offering to speak to a Georgian seaman's ghost.

'You could try,' he said doubtfully.

'If I told them you were born in Falmouth would that help?'

'Who knows?' said Jack.

'How do I contact them?'

'Go down to my workroom late one night and shout, "Light along, Jem Shrubsole, to the Cornish chippie's workshop",' he said, 'You never know it might work.'

'What do I say if he appears?'

'Tell him to take a note you'll write to his captain telling him what I've told you.'

I made my way to his house and, after asking Jack's wife if I could use his workroom, I shouted out for Jem feeling very foolish. As I expected nothing happened and then a shadow fell across the desk I was sitting by...

'Jem Shrubsole at your service, Sir,' he said, making his obedience.

'I have a note for your captain here,' I said. 'Please see he gets it at once.'

'You bide here a moment, Sir,' he said. 'And I'll get it to him.'

I waited for what seemed a long time and then he reappeared.

'All shipshape, Sir,' he said. 'Captain's gone ashore but left a note for Mr Barker, First Lieutenant who's in charge. He'll look after you. Hold hard Sir, and I'll have you there in a jiffy.'

The room darkened and when the light resumed I was in a small wooden cabin facing a young officer sitting at an untidy desk.

'This has gone quite far enough,' I said.

Giles Granville-Barker, First Lieutenant, looked up wearily from the mass of paperwork littering his desk.

'Damn shipyard squabs chipping my paintwork, it's a regular Bartholomew's Fair out there,' he said. 'What was it, Sir? Oh yes, the captain left a note.'

He rummaged around and found a dogeared scrap of paper which looked as if someone had used it to mop up some coffee. At least I hoped it was coffee.

'You'd better speak to Cyrus Oldshore,' he said. 'Captain of Olde Crankie, third gun on the starboard side, he's your man.' He tilted his chair back and shouted very loudly over his shoulder up the companion way. 'Light along Cyrus Oldshore to Captain's Day Cabin.'

There was the sound of heavy boots and a bulky weathered, middle-aged man clumped down the stairs and stood uneasily before the lieutenant, twisting his woollen hat.

'You cover early twenty-first century don't you, Oldshore?' said the Lieutenant.

'Aye, Sir,' said Cyrus. 'Man and boy these many years past.'

'And who handles... "Cornish Shipbuilders"?' asked the officer, referring to the captain's note.'

'North or the more *Sutherly* ones, Sir?' said Cyrus, with a helpful smile, revealing a mouthful of blackened teeth.

'Well I don't know, man,' said the Lieutenant. 'Surely one man can cover both, dammit. They're virtually the same.'

'Never in life, Sir,' said. Cyrus. 'A world of difference, beggin' your pardon. Southerly's are placid souls from little creek-like places and sheltered coves, whereas *North*, why they're right in the teeth of Atlantic gales most like and facing 'Mericee where them renegade British calling themselves 'Mericans fester and foment trouble.'

'If I want a geography lesson,' said the Lieutenant. 'I'll ask for it, you impudent dog.'

'Well, Sir, which it to be?' said Cyrus amiably, not in the least put out.

'South, damn your eyes,' said Giles. 'Now take this gentleman to the wardroom and tell Pillick I said you might go there to help him. And report back at eight bells. Now get out and leave me to get on with all this.'

Then, recalling he had a guest, he checked himself, looked up wearily from his Shipyard dockets and said, 'Good-day to you, Sir, I trust I have been of service.'

We left the room and made our way to the empty wardroom where we sat down.

'Is he always like that?' I asked.

'In port they're like that,' said Cyrus. 'Proper seamen, that is. That's civil for him. He knows Cornwall like the back of his hand – he was just letting some wind spill from his sails. Known him since he was seized up over the barrel of a gun for a caning they calls "kissing the gunner's daughter". Just a little squeak he was then, come on something marvellous. Now, Sir, how can I assist you?'

'You or one of your… colleagues,' I said. 'Have been visiting a good friend of mine who makes ships.'

'More like *boatbuilding* then, Sir?' said Cyrus. 'In a small way of things – crafts of modest dimensions, like?'

'Smallish, but nothing modest about the quality of his workmanship,' I protested.

'Hold hard, young Sir,' he smiled. 'Take in a reef or two – no need to get your top-hamper in a tangle.'

'He's been quite ill,' I said. 'With a jaw problem.'

'Poor gentl'man,' said Cyrus. '"Gimlet Gunner" Williams, Captain "Widow Maker" third port-side gun's a rare hand, if *extraction's* needed, Sir.'

'I'm afraid it's more drastic than that,' I said.

'Chips the carpenter or the sailmaker might make him a little *oral support*,' said Cyrus. 'Like for dead shipmates to keep their gobs tight afore heaving them over the side.'

'Kindly meant,' I said. 'But I think my friend would prefer a more *delicate* approach. Nothing too sudden or violent.'

'Is your shipmate a personage of *letters,* Sir.'

'Yes, I suppose so, in a way,' I said.' Is that relevant?'

'Brain work and suchlike, if he's one for the books, Sir.'

'Can we move on,' I said. 'He feels he's being threatened with physical violence. I believe there was mention of a marling spike…'

'In what connection may I enquire, Sir?' said Sam.

'A sharp tap on the noggin with the aforesaid implement,' I said.

'There you are, Sir,' said Cyrus patiently 'A sharp tap! What I was getting at – the right remedy for a bookish gentleman to relieve the pain in that *overstretched* noggin of his.'

'With a marling spike?" I protested.

'Never in life, Sir,' protested Cyrus. 'A belayin'pin like as not, but never a *marling* spike. Not for *noggin* bashing. Not Bristol fashion, any tide.' He shook his head sadly at the outrageous use of such an object for such a purpose.

'I'm glad to hear it,' I said. 'No violence, please.'

'Bless you, no Sir,' said Cyrus. 'But a sharp *tap* on the noggin as been known to work wonders on injured shipmates.'

'I don't think that would work with him,' I said.

'Not even a *light* tap?' he said, hopefully.

'Have you a surgeon on board I might talk to?'

'We have, Sir, a right one he is too,' said Sam, with a smile. 'Likely he'll be aboard taking his customary nap at this time of day. I take your drift, Sir – you would rest more easy like if he was to administer the aforesaid tiny tap, himself.'

'Just let me speak to him, please,' I said.

'I'll pass the word for him, Sir,' he said and bellowed up the stairs, 'Dr Manurin to the wardroom.'

'How can I help you, Sir,' said a large, florid gentleman wedging himself sideways into the room. 'I perceive in you a *sluggishness* that suggests the benefit of immediate medical attention, and a slight adjustment to the excess volume of your blood will speedily restore you to health. I charge civilians by the leech hour.'

'My friend, who is a naval architect in a small way, has upset the entire British Georgian Navy by using shipbuilding techniques unheard of in your era,' I said.

'Ah, that pantomime,' he said, disappointed.

'And he is being threatened by a form of physical abuse with a belaying pin for doing so. He is not well at present and I must ask you to use your good offices, Sir, to counsel your emissaries not to…'

'Indulge in any cranial massage. But before we leave the other subject perhaps you would prefer your phlebotomy through a *veinous* incision. As luck would have it I have a scalpel on my person We lack but a bowl.'

'No! No!' I cried. 'Damn your inclinations! Suggest some other remedial action for my friend, short of physical violence.'

'As neither blood-letting for you nor cranial percussion for your friend appeal to you, Sir,' said the surgeon, coldly. 'The window of medicinal options available to me is rapidly closing.'

'Cyrus, let me speak to the lieutenant,' I said wearily.

'If I might counsel another option, Sir,' he said, forgetting to be *foremast* and improving his articulation. 'Get the gentleman to depart from fancy elaborations and devilish tricks and eschew his newfangled ways. Then all will be well and...'

'How can I persuade him?'

'Why bless you, Sir. If he steers a right course then the high seas and naval world are his oyster. All our resources and ships will be his to command. He has only to raise his colours and say the word.'

'I will stand as a guarantor for him – I know he wouldn't want it any other way.'

'Then he will be a true Cornishman in the Court of King George,' said Cyrus, smiling, broadly.

'All will be well, and all manner of rigging and planking and caulking and... other things will be well,' I said, getting into the spirit of things.

★ ★ ★

Jack agreed at once, as I knew he would, and I sent word to Jem and Cyrus assuring them of his complete co-operation. I don't know what happened then, but I've often observed that, summer and winter, my friend Jack possesses a weather-beaten sort of complexion even though he lives in rain-soaked England and wouldn't dream of going to a tanning parlour. Any more than he would have sought out a gym to develop that rolling gait of his which suggests a life containing some irregular *motion* and not entirely spent on dry land either!

BRIEF ENCOUNTER

G rayston Elliott was a forty-year-old American accountant. He spoke only English, peppered his meagre vocabulary with technical terms, seldom went to the movies, didn't read novels and had never scanned a single line of poetry. He distrusted the unexpected and was uneasy with those he couldn't relate to or understand which included women, innumerate persons and artists. He was the last person you might expect to deeply experience what the French call a *"coup de foudre"*.

Although often taken to mean love at first sight this can also refer to an extreme reaction to a sudden, unforeseen event. But the intensity of Grayston's *coup* meant that it was heavily skewed towards the former– the delicious delight of the first encounter of kindred souls rather than simply an unexpected incident. And although initially fleeting unlike many other *coups* it had a lasting conclusion for at least one of the parties involved.

Grayston was an East Coast urbanite to the core. As an only child he'd lived all his life in the big city and his schooling was largely conducted on concrete floors behind high brick walls. College was much the same followed by routine accountancy in a large local corporation where he was considered to be reliable, conscientious and unpromotable. And from early middle age he lived alone in an apartment left to him by his late parents who were already advanced in years when he was born.

He was content with his lot because his circumstances allowed him to do what he loved most which was, rather surprisingly, nurturing his deep love of the natural world. As you might expect he did this at one remove from reality by learning in the library all he could about nature, its inhabitants and their behaviour. And although careful with money he'd a flair for financial speculation on the stock exchange which would have astonished his employers. With the extra income generated by this activity he bought a log cabin in a remote northern part of the state in which he lived and spent as much time there as his work permitted. That was nothing like enough and to his delight, shared by most of his colleagues, he negotiated a deal with his company allowing him very generous unpaid leave of absence.

Living full time in his cabin he blossomed, rejoicing in its natural setting and sustained by frugal self-sufficiency. If there was anyone who knew or cared about him they would have considered it remarkable for such an urbanite to be so much at home alone there, in that great forest stretching far northwards towards the icy wastes of the Arctic tundra. But there he prospered, calmed by the deep silence around him, spending his days observing nature going about its business of living, although indifferent to the hunting and killing that such a life also entailed.

In theory he'd already mastered most of the descriptions of natural life and now he began carefully logging the behaviour of the flora and fauna around him. Building on a foundation of received wisdom, he classified everything he saw, quietly confident that his small world of animals, birds and insects had never before been so well described, recorded or so thoroughly catalogued. He'd no wish to communicate his enjoyment to others, content to hug the experience to himself, feeling that sharing would somehow diminish his own pleasure.

His great regret was that although his research revealed there should be bears in the forest, he had never even seen any evidence of one let alone a sighting. And how he yearned for the chance! He never carried firearms but had pepper spray and knew what to do with it if he was attacked but without use it lay forgotten in a drawer.

And so imagine his delight when one day whilst observing the behaviour of wood ants under his favourite tree he was approached by a very large brown bear. Some time ago it had been airlifted from an urban area where it had developed considerable expertise in opening food containers and feasting on scraps left around by careless townsfolk. Here in its natural habitat the bear was constantly hungry and ill-tempered for it liked everything about its life in the town and cared nothing for wild woods where everything was so damned difficult to get to eat.

Grayston saw the animal but was not concerned, quite the opposite. His heart gave a great leap of joy for in front of him stood the most important missing piece of his great outdoor jigsaw. An undoubted *coup de foudre* for both of them. For a similar sentiment was coursing through the veins of the disgruntled bear and suffusing its stomach lining with aching and longing. At last, it said, this awful wilderness is offering you the opportunity of combining deep desire with its imminent satisfaction.

After he'd devoured as much of Grayston as he could manage the newly plump and happy bear slept, dreaming of lovely rows of well-lit streets awash with sweet, delicious food. But when it awoke the magic was gone, for he was back in the accursed forest with nothing to eat without guile and effort. He survived until winter on berries and the ill or old creature he could catch, but never ceased to yearn in his rare moments of leisure for the rich pastures of urban life. And when he hibernated it was to these Elysian fields that his dreamlife led him.

In his uncomplicated ursine way, he had a very special dream reliving the moment his feral heart stood still in that magic moment when he met Grayston. And even in the brief hectic moments before his final exit the accountant would surely have rejoiced in the knowledge that he would forever remain in his beloved woods. Although it must be said that in an ideal world and with more time to plan the event, his departure would have been rather less messy and considerably more *orderly* than it turned out to be.

THE LAST CHARGE OF THE MAWDDACH MAURAUDERS

Following the "realignment" of the United States into four Great Regional States the United Kingdom followed suit with its constituent countries. In both cases civil war resulted, but in contrast to the US which were never reunited, a lasting truce was established in United Britain and hostilities ceased after only two months of "phoney war" in which not a shot was fired. However, pockets of resistance remained – not unlike the case of the Japanese soldiers taking refuge in the jungle during the Second World War who believed it was still going on many years after it had finished.

In Britain one such instance occurred when a Welsh guerrilla unit left their base in the Brecon Beacons after two years living off the land. Nicknamed the "Pocket Ghurkhas" because of their carefully chosen small size, their appearance at a golf tournament at the Royal Lytham & St Anne's Golf Club led to the so-called "Battle of the Links", marking the end of a largely forgotten conflict.

This is their story – a drama documentary pieced together by a team of investigative journalists from documentary evidence and scraps overheard in various public houses following the incident. To give the narrative authenticity it contains the actual real-time dialogue of what was spoken in the run-up to the historic encounter. Those unacquainted with the reality of combat may find some of the details upsetting.

★ ★ ★

'They won't use *drones* on us, will they, Sarge?' asked little Thomas Two, when the column of men stopped for a rest in a ditch by the side of a wood. Sergeant Rhys, finishing off his emergency rations after their early ten o'clock start didn't reply. In good time he'd look up "Drones" in his well-thumbed Canadian Army Infantryman's 1983 Handbook but for now his mind was more on easing off his uncomfortable desert boots. They'd never fitted properly, hardly surprising given that he'd wrenched them off the feet of a dead jihadist whilst dodging flying bullets in a fierce firefight in a desert engagement. At least that's what he implied when questioned about them, whereas he'd actually got them cheap from a Port Talbot retail outlet.

'This isn't going to be a picnic,' he said to his corporal, Thomas One, wincing as he rubbed the reddened flesh of his naked foot. His words went largely unheeded for his second-in-command, a fifty a day man, was bent double coughing as the injection of fresh air inflamed his labouring lungs.

'No sandwiches and Scotch eggs, then, Sarge?' cried Jenkins Three, looking up from his natural exertions behind a nearby bush.

'And no jelly to follow!' Dai the Dim, their Sniper shouted out suddenly in that unexpected way of his and Griffiths the Gonads, studying selfie shots of himself wearing red satin knickers on his head on a distant Choir Outing to Cardiff's city centre, was startled out of a pleasant reverie.

'You shut your mouth, Dimmo,' he shouted. 'And you keep that bloody fancy rifle of yours out of my way.' He hated Dai's assumed but unproven marksmanship almost as much as he coveted the weapon.

'Shut up, shut *up* the lot of you,' said the sergeant, pulling on his boots. He reached for his pack from which he drew an Ordnance Survey map with the price tag in pre-decimal currency still attached. He beckoned to Jenkins Three to come and bend over so that he could spread the map across his back. Then he called the corporal over.

'See here, Tommo, this is more or less where we are,' he said. 'And *this* is more than likely where we regroup before the offensive.'

Thomas One gazed at the map for some time without speaking. At last he said, 'Upside down, it is.'

The sergeant removed the map from Jenkin's back and kicked his arse.

'Come with me,' he said to the corporal. 'And keep your head down.'

They pushed past the rest of their platoon treading heavily on Dai the Deli's delicately arranged sandwiches and moved along the ditch to where the land rose slightly. The sergeant peered over the bank and, after parting some stinging nettles, motioned to Thomas to join him in appraising the undulating landscape.

'Observe the strip of green beside that copse,' he said. 'That's the key to our advance.'

'We'll meet a few of those getting near where the action is, I'm thinking,' muttered Thomas, whose hearing aid had fallen off during the night.

'"Copse" not "corpse", you idiot *gwirion!*' said Rhys.

'Both dead though,' said Thomas. 'Eh, Sarge?'

'Oh, never mind,' said Rhys wearily

'Near going into action?' said Thomas. 'Time for a tot of rum apiece and a few words from you. Don't mention drones, though.'

'What's all this about bloody *drones?*' said Rhys. 'A heavily armed platoon like us in the peak of condition, state of the art hardware, rapid response trained and suddenly everyone's on about plastic kid's toys!'

'But you won't mention them, will you, Sarge?'

'No I bloody won't and not just to please you,' he said. 'Now just let's get on with our job!'

They retraced their steps pausing only to seek out and apply dock leaves to the sergeant's hands now blotchy with nettle rash and when they rejoined the platoon they deployed the men in a ditch overlooking the terrain they'd surveyed.

'Over by those trees is a sandy dip,' whispered Rhys, pointing. 'That's where we'll *muster* before the thrust that'll punch a hole through their defences. Now get your backsides down there and keep low. Stay close to me, Jones, I'll want you near me with your bazooka, so make your bloody self useful, for a change.'

'Yes, Sarge,' said Jones the Joker, with his wide smile, shocking teeth and terrible breath. 'Any chance of some ammo?'

'Ammo or no ammo, that's what the foe will see you carrying into battle,' said Rhys. '"Shock and awe", modern warfare tactics.'

'What's that mean?' said little Thomas Two.

'It means, boyo, carrying a bloody great empty metal tube half-way round England,' said Jones.

'You shut up!' rasped the sergeant. 'Now you lot do what you're told, and get down there.'

The men emerged from the ditch and, bending double, ran down the hill, jumped into the pit and spread themselves around the sides of the depression. The sergeant joined them and peered cautiously over the sandy ridge fringed by brittle marram grass. Particles of fine sand got everywhere with maddening ease, clogging the nostrils and irritating throats. The corporal's heroic attempts to stem his renewed coughing, threatened not only to deprive them of the element of surprise but render him permanently unfit for combat.

Then Rhys remembered he'd forgotten his field glasses, which it was well known he'd prised from the stiffening fingers of a dead terrorist officer on a clandestine mission. Recalling that Dai had a telescopic sight on his rifle he told him to come forward.

'I can't see anything, this sand's all over the bloody shop,' he said to the sharpshooter when he'd wriggled up to join him. 'See if you can spot anything with that lens of yours.'

Dai aimed his good eye at his rifle's sight.

'Funny old country this, Sarge,' he said. 'Little hills and bumps all over with poles and flags marking something. *Mines,* like as not. No one around but they could be hiding, mind. Sneaky English.'

'Maybe they withdrew after the great Scottish advance, like that boy from the village told us last night,' said the sergeant. 'He said the English took one look at the Jocks and scampered away like a bunch of scared rabbits.'

'Believed him, did you?' said Dai, 'I'm not so sure. Strange that boy was, kept laughing and sniggering at nothing. A bit touched I'd say.'

'I didn't notice, but he was the first native we've spoken to since we left the secret briefing in Eglwyswrw,' said Rhys. 'And it doesn't do to underestimate the English when their backs are to the wall.'

'They can't hold out much longer, can they, Sarge?' said Stephens the Sapper who'd struggled up to join them and look over the brow of the hill.

'Who gave you permission to get up here, you little runt?' said Rhys, as the tiny ex-miner scrabbling for a footing, sent sand cascading down around him.

'If there's any *digging* to do come nightfall,' said Stephens. 'I'll be welcome then, to be sure.'

'To be sure,' said Dai, mimicking his accent. 'That'll be a first, look you.'

'Shut *up*, both of you,' hissed the sergeant 'No one's going anywhere until we see what's in front of us.' He turned and whispered loudly down to two men huddled at the base of the depression. 'You bloody Yorkshire tykes, get up here.' There were sounds of a brief struggle and two wiry men wearing flat caps, one with a walleye and the other with a surgical boot were pushed up the slope to where he was laying.

'You creep round our flanks one left and one right, and then get back and report what you've seen,' said Rhys. 'And don't let anyone see either of you.'

'I'm not bloody going. I'm a non-combatant, a prisoner of war, me,' protested the first. 'At least that's what everyone keeps telling me.'

'How does "RIP" on your tombstone appeal to you?' said the sergeant. 'We've got enough bullets to see you both off and no questions asked. Now get your sorry arses off like I said, and don't try any funny business or our sniper here will get a bit of practice!'

The men shuffled off and were soon lost to sight. The sergeant had no fears that they might try to escape for they had nowhere to go. He relaxed for a moment.

'Got a fag?' he whispered to Corporal Thomas who obliged, and together they drew heavily on their home-made roll-ups made of what smelt like dried dung. They'd been travelling by night for days in enemy territory and hadn't risked raiding shops for cigarettes.

'Ever get to London, Sarge?' asked Thomas, inhaling with a grimace of pain. 'Before the obliteration, mind.'

'No, never really fancied going. All foreigners and strange talk, I heard. Too late now, what with the French invasion, like that kid said last night. I went to Penbryn once, mind. Well, almost.'

'Nice town so they say,' Thomas exhaled, with a sound like sandpaper being rubbed vigorously on a sheet of rusty corrugated iron. 'For a big place, that is.'

They fell silent each with his own thoughts, and after a while there was a rustling as the men returned from their flanks and reported that the enemy had appeared. Very carefully, the sergeant raised his head above the rim of the depression. In the middle distance he saw a large crowd of what looked like prisoners crowded together behind barriers and gave a hiss of disapproval at the brutality. In front of the huddled masses he saw two huge, strangely clothed figures standing looking down at the grass at their feet holding weapons with cruelly curved metallic ends. They seemed harmless enough, little unsuspecting that near at hand was a trained well-armed militia poised to disarm and take them prisoners.

Judging from their giant stature and rounded vowels they must be English, he thought. *Strange that these defeated people seemed to have no cares in the world.* It was as if they hadn't heard that vast numbers of their countrymen had been incarcerated in the Home Counties Reservation controlled by the Pan Cwmric Federation. Or feared the righteous wrath of those who'd vowed to wage total war until the last English syllable was banished for ever from the British Islands? *But his not to reason why,* he thought, and with a certain confidence in the outcome addressed the men in a loud whisper.

'Minimum force,' he said. 'Don't want anything too *messy.* Better fix bayonets, though, just in case.'

'What do we fix them to, Sarge?' asked Jenkins Three. 'We've only got two rifles.'

'And only one bayonet because Dai... we was going to tell you, Sarge, honest,' said Griffiths.

'I've got a Swiss army knife with a corkscrew. Could fix that nice,' said Jenkins Three. 'In the right hands...' he said, meaningfully.

Several of the others nodded, and Dai the Deli whistled under his breath.

'Anyone got any *string*,' said Jenkins.

'Shut up, shut up, shut *up*,' said the Sergeant. 'Mano a Mano, it is then.'

'What's that mean?' said Sapper.

'"Hand to hand", and them with *drones* most like,' said Thomas Two.

'Never bloody mind, just grab the buggers, and release the prisoners,' said Rhys. 'Then it's behind the barbed wire if we can find some, interrogation, a tot of rum all round for us and back to Trwyn-y-Bwa before the week is out.'

'Then on to the Pan-Cymric Rally at Bryn Henllan before the Welsh Fleet sails for America and does there what we've done here,' breathed Dai.

'And for all the English-speaking nations after we've done with *them*,' shouted out Dai the Dim. 'Purifying the world's vocabulary.'

'Or die trying!' shouted Rhys.

The men hauled themselves over the ridge screaming '*Y ddraig goch ddyry cychwynet cymru am byth!*' and rushed forward with Thomas and the unfurled Red Dragon flag billowing above in step with his coughing. The enemy looked up curiously as the gaggle of tiny, bullet-headed munchkins suddenly appeared from behind a bunker and ran towards them over the putting green gibbering fiercely.

The encounter was intense but decisive, for the English enemy, surprised at first and savagely hacked around the shins in that first devastating onrush, fell back and used their woods to fell the first rank, checked the rest with their middle irons and completely routed the rest with their putters.

The Interim Welsh Government, contacted in the Caribbean where protracted peace negotiations were continuing, unaware of the attack suggested that after receiving immediate medical aid the sedated bodies of the unit should be air lifted by helicopter to the Brecon Beacons and the bodies gently released back into the wild.

Some time after their return the platoon sergeant reported to the High Command of the Cwmric Military Academy over the tobacconist's shop in Felindre Farchog. The men were then tasked with covert surveillance operations carried out whilst delivering English newspapers under the direction of "P" known to the outside world as simply "Mr Patel".

And so ended the last known infantry charge on British soil, a feat immortalised by the crossed golf clubs fore and aft on the cap badge of the Mawddach Maurauders and worn with immense pride to this very day.

AN APPETITE FOR LOVE

'What do you feel about animal rights campaigns?' I asked Tom, a good friend who was also a university lecturer in animal behaviour.

'There's no doubt that many animals possess the sensory apparatus that should equip them to feel similar sensations to humans,' he said, with the usual scientific caution.

'Any evidence they have *emotions*?'

'Ah, much more tricky,' he said. 'Because people always want to explain animal behaviour through the prism of our motivation.'

'As if they were human.'

'Yes it's called "Anthropomorphism",' he said. 'I've always thought that pet devotion can be explained by reward seeking rather than genuine "love". Whatever that is.'

'Like the conditioned reflexes of Pavlov's dogs,' I said.

'Possibly – but living things are notoriously complex, and we know so little about even simple creatures like spiders,' he said. 'Perhaps rudimentary nervous systems disguise undreamt of emotional capabilities.'

'Surely observing behaviour, reveals *something*?' I said.

'To a point, but we still tend to interpret what we see in the light of human experience,' he said. 'Let's see – give me an example of what you think of as an advanced or refined human emotion.'

'Self-sacrifice,' I said, after a while.

He beckoned to me to follow him into his study and once there pointed to a large glass cylinder on his desk.

'Look inside this jar,' he said. 'And witness fussy Belinda and someone I introduced her to some hours ago, who I've called Marcus.'

'I can't see much in there,' I said. 'Just some twigs.'

'Look more carefully.'

'Oh yes, there's a stick insect inside. No two – they're mating I think.'

'They are praying mantises,' he said. 'She's been very choosey about her partner and has rejected lots of males, but little Marcus seems to have made the cut. Bless him.'

'Do you think there are emotions at play here or merely instincts?' I said.

'Who can tell? Let's watch the behaviour of Marcus and we might see him exhibit what might be described as an example of the so-called refined emotion of self-sacrifice for their issue.'

'I almost feel guilty watching them,' I said, and he smiled at the thought.

★ ★ ★

From their first meeting Belinda and Marcus had felt an irresistible urge to surrender to an overpowering mutual desire that could not be denied or delayed. The beautiful Belinda and Marcus in his prime, full of vigour and virility, sensing that she, who had rejected others, had saved herself for one such as he. And now, at last, they were together.

He suspected it was stolen bliss and harm might be lurking in wait for him but so overwhelming was his passion for her that such a risk he set at nought. What price caution to the strength of their love? Let the whole world come in arms and they would prevail. He clasped her in his strong arms and drew her closely to his hard body and she yielded utterly and eventually it was done.

After the searing heat of union, she looked affectionately at him wrapped in his post-coital bliss. And then another feeling overwhelmed her, a terrible savage lust for the life they had created, a raging appetite, insistent and undeniable. He felt her body move and saw her seized by such a sensation of fresh longing that her arms had released him and she seemed to be praying in an ecstasy of desire – the craving desire to give to their unborn child the start in life that only a well fed mother could provide.

Then he understood, but he moved just a fraction too late...

NOT WAVING BUT DROWNING

'*How did it come to this?*' Peter Swift groaned, desperately gripping the swaying mast as more seawater surged over the waterlogged catamaran in the heavy swell. And a voice in his head replied, '*Where else but in Berto's bar?*'

Oh yes – he remembered the bar in Isla Mujeres where he'd met Jeff, the man with no other name and the rum punches flowing in that seedy place where no one cared if you'd had a breakdown or why you lived in a grubby little hotel all day and drank all night. He'd never even heard of the port before he left the United States but it's easy to find if you start at Corpus Christi, Texas, go over the border into Mexico and follow the coast until you reach Veracruz. Then, skirting the waters of the Bay of Campeche, you'll find Cancun on the Yucatan peninsula and thirteen miles off the coast lies the Isla, the nearest point in Mexico to Key West, Florida.

'*Oh Jesus, it's turning over!*' Peter breathed as the catamaran heeled heavily before plunging down into a deep trough. Then it righted and Jeff's words came back to him.

'A cat's virtually unsinkable. And if you know how to sail one you can easily get to Cuba, it's only 100 nautical miles to Cabo San Antonio.'

'I haven't done much sailing,' said Peter.

'I've found a small cat I've named *"Nirvana"* in a local yard,' Jeff said. 'They often have an old one for sale and I want to get used to it before taking people out game fishing. I'm going to sail it to Cuba, sneak in near the Cabo and I'm looking for someone to help me crew it over. A few days sailing, a pleasant trip and a good time in Cuba. What about it?'

Peter mumbled he'd think about it. But after the tanned, bearded Jeff had spoken of his Atlantic crossings and showed him his IYT Yachtmaster's Offshore Certificate, he wavered. And when he outlined the route on a scrap of paper as if he was plotting an aircraft's flight path it was clear he knew what he was doing. So Peter agreed but only after making it clear he'd leave the sailing and other arrangements to Jeff.

A few days later the Nirvana sailed on the ebbtide after a last-minute hitch with the on-board radio – vital before the introduction of smart phones and all seemed well as they glided out on the ebbtide. Their first day at sea was uneventful, although Peter, who had felt nervous after seeing the size and condition of the cat was even more anxious when they were out of sight of land. In the open sea the current entering the Gulf of Mexico from the Caribbean is testing for a small craft and the sluggish steering soon suggested that they were in for trouble. And, as they settled ever lower in the water even to Peter's inexperienced eyes, you could hear the hulls moving loosely and grinding against the central part of the boat.

'No problem, we're already nearer Cuba than Mexico,' said Jeff. 'It may take us a while but we'll make it OK. We still have an engine.'

'But we were going to *sail* across,' said Peter. 'And only use the engine for getting into Cabo. What happens when the fuel's gone?'

'We've got a radio,' said Jeff, impatiently, showing him the Coast Guard number to ring and how to pinpoint their location from the radar. Peter, who wished he had more confidence in their equipment, listened in silence.

In spite of his apparent calm Jeff worked hard to secure the hulls and in the heaving sea he overbalanced and fell heavily striking his head on the deck. Peter, after making him as comfortable as he could, called up the US Coast Guard, gave them their current location and asked for immediate help. Shortly after their radio set failed and all he could do was look after the unconscious Jeff, grip the mast and act as lookout to guide their rescuers and cursing his decision to come in the first place.

You can imagine his relief when he saw the Coast Guard plane on the horizon. It circled low over them several times with a co-pilot filming the cat before they dipped their wings and disappeared over the horizon to the north. Several hours later when no rescue boat had arrived Peter almost gave up hope, but then a container ship spotted them, launched a tender and took them to Galveston

* * *

In the flurry of their arrival in Galveston Port Jeff disappeared and Peter, after his ordeal and with no credentials appeared to suffer almost total memory loss. Busy Customs and Border Patrol Agency staff referred him to the psychological unit of another branch of the Department of Homeland Security who, unknown to Peter, worked closely with their security colleagues on cases of "unsecured entry and possible border violations". It was not unknown that memory loss was a device used by some with good reasons to avoid detection whilst on the sacred soil of the United States of America.

It was made clear to Peter that although he would receive help, for the present he would be housed in a hostel run by the Border Force where his movements would be carefully monitored. And it was here, in a small, spartan room that a fresh-faced young man called Lou interviewed him, several days later.

Lou, actually as hard as nails, specialised in engaging friendliness and questioned him closely noting from his East Coast accent that he was American. But as to his name, birthplace, family background, education and subsequent career he drew a blank. And, after two days of frustration, he changed tactics.

'If we re-enact the final stages of your voyage that might conceivably yield some hard data and provide us with some *traction* to your past history,' he said. 'Let us strive together to reclaim your identity.'

'You told me that I contacted the Coast Guard Service,' said Peter guardedly.

'A good place to start,' said Lou, and arrangements were made for Peter to speak to the operators in Hillard Street, Galveston who would have been on duty at the time.

Having identified the likely operators, Lou spoke privately to their supervisor who cleared with management that the operator could answer reasonable questions as long as it didn't interfere with any work in hand.

'Now over to you, Sir,' he said to Peter.

'Have you a precise record of our conversation?' he asked the operator.

'We routinely record all communication,' said a voice at the other end.

'So you'll have a record of the date and time I contacted you.'

'I didn't say that, but I can check when I have a moment.'

'If I contact you at a more suitable time will that help?' said Peter.

'Mid morning in the week is always a better time to ring an overstretched service such as ours than now at 4.55 on a Friday,' was the reply. 'And I am momentarily otherwise engaged at present but I will ask my supervisor to help you.'

'How may I be of assistance?' said another voice, after a longish pause.

'I wanted confirmation that I spoke to one of your colleagues after making a Mayday call,' he said.

'Where you given a contact log number?' they replied.

'Not that I remember.'

'That will mean a delay while we search. What was the exact nature of your contact?'

Peter explained the situation and there was a pause while they found the original enquiry that showed a call had been logged and a plane had been sent.

'So what happened to the rescue boat?' Peter asked.

'You were outside our territorial waters. We had no legal obligation to instigate or effect a recovery scenario,' was the reply.

'But I understood we were *sinking*?'

'"In some apparent distress", according to the flight log,' was the reply.

'With *water* lapping around my ankles!'

'Sub-terminal Inundation Status was the assessment, Sir,' she said.

'No wonder we nearly drowned!' Peter said, heatedly.

'Please moderate your tone, Sir,' said the operator, 'I'm trying to be helpful.'

'I merely pointed out that I was told that our decks were awash with most of the contents of the Gulf of Mexico and a large dash of the Caribbean.'

'Our pilot is extremely experienced in sea-borne rescue operations,' said the supervisor. 'And did not detect any life-threatening aspects of your situation.'

'But did they get a good look at us?' Peter asked.

'They circled your craft at several hundred feet,' said the voice, with a tinge of impatience.

'Why? Had they left their glasses at home?' Peter replied

'They were quite properly trying to establish the identity

of your vessel to check your details from your duly registered "Intended Destination" input.'

'Didn't the skipper on our boat do that?'

'Apparently not, Sir,' said the supervisor severely. 'Inexperienced sailors often endanger others without informing the proper authorities and expect the American taxpayer to cover the cost of sending out a rescue boat.'

'He probably thought we were Mexicans sneaking into the States through the back door,' said Peter. 'Or maybe drug runners sending you a Mayday in broad daylight!'

'Sir, I would urge you to avoid such accusations,' said the supervisor. 'On a happier note, you'll be proud to know that you appear in a short scene in our promotional video which was completed shortly after we contacted your fine vessel.'

'So you were *filming* us for a video!'

'Yes, *Sir*!'

'Why?'

'So that the good folks who help fund us can appreciate the perils of our "Seek and Save Rescue Service".'

'You must be joking!' said Peter.

'No indeed, Sir,' the supervisor. 'May we put you down for a copy, discounted in your case, of course. We will be pleased to defray the postage.'

At this point Peter looked at Lou and said, 'I really can't stand any more of this.'

Lou looked disappointed but nodded and thanked the supervisor who said, 'You're welcome. Now you have a good day,' and rang off.

Lou suggested that his intervention had reached a point where he believed only further observation and interaction with a dedicated skilled practitioner over a longer period would yield results. A temporary stay visa of four months was therefore granted to Peter during which time he would continue to be housed in a government hostel, receive a basic living allowance but have to attend a counselling session daily during that period. His case would then be reviewed.

But during the night he disappeared for good from the official radar of the United States' Border Agency.

★ ★ ★

So had Peter really lost his memory and had he something to hide? Of course he hadn't and of course he did. He had not lost his memory but was desperate to avoid detection in the US for a number of smuggling offences over many years. Indeed that was the very reason why he was hiding in Mexico in the first place. The Feds were closing in on him particularly the agencies in Texas. So he jumped at the idea of a trip to Cuba with Jeff as he planned to slip away, hide on the island for some time and then try to get back to the States via the Florida Keys with a new identity

The last thing he wanted was to be filmed by the rescue plane. Unfortunately for him the US Coast Guards were alerted to the *possibility* it was him by an extremely smart analyst reviewing the rescue plane's film footage. But they needed more positive confirmation that it was indeed him after photo forensics found that the grainy image from the plane couldn't provide that. And so a rescue boat was sent to get him on US soil. But then the tanker from Panama picked them up before the rescue boat could arrive.

For a Federal Indictment the authorities needed more evidence about Peter and decided to keep him in the States after his so-called loss of memory to see if he might betray anything during therapy. The lie about the filming for a promotional video was to reassure him that his fears about being recognised from the plane were groundless.

So what about Jeff who disappeared? The first thing about him was that he had no intention of taking Peter to Cuba – he was heading for Key West and US territory. But two things thwarted that plan – the poor choice of catamaran and his genuine accident. Barring that he would have nursed the ailing cat to Florida. But why did he want to go there so much? And what happened to him?

By sailing there he would have got Peter onto US soil and that was what he and his boss, the Director of a US Coast Guard Special Services Unit wanted very badly. If, of course, there had been such a person and if such a body existed. In the much-protected United States there are so many agencies concerning Homeland Security that inevitably their activities sometimes overlap and often neither side knows of the other's involvement.

And Jeff's current whereabouts? Try any seedy bar somewhere around the Caribbean and you'll likely find him chatting away and making friends, because he's easy to talk to and nice to meet. And he knows just *everyone*. He *might* even be drinking with Peter who he *may* have recruited into a clandestine surveillance unit like the other miscreants he'd turned from poachers into gamekeepers. But obviously only if a body like that existed, which of course it didn't then, doesn't now and never will.

FREE SPIRITS

When I got a thought transmission telling me to wind up my current assignment and go to Earth it meant adjusting a complicated schedule. Were I human I would be displeased and annoyed. But I'm a high-made cyborg and we don't react so illogically.

Like most of my cohort I'd no liking for anything purely organic but I always got tasks involving biologicals because in my manufacture a larger than normal amount of vestigial DNA was accidentally retained in my neural inputs. Were I capable of negative emotion I'd be ashamed of those lingering traces of humanity and so I hardly leapt at being told to visit Earth.

'For what reason do you wish me to go there?' I thought.

'To find out what you can about primitive human manned space programmes.'

'For what reason?' I thought, back.

'Because a craft manned by humans in deep hibernation has just left the Galaxy.'

'That is impossible.'

'It cannot be because we have tracked its progress and it has passed beyond our boundary intact.'

'What are my orders?'

'Radiation levels are low enough at last to permit physical terrestrial exploration. You are to examine the origin of the craft and the culture from which it came to see if there is an explanation for this anomaly. That is all.'

★ ★ ★

I took a passage on a tender from Port Titan taking a relief crew to a solar orbiter and used one of their shuttles to descend to Earth's surface. As an advanced cyborg I could adjust my metabolism to "fully autonomous" using the shuttle as a base, and as a human-sized sphere although lacking arms or legs on my anti-grav mobile platform with its flexible probes I was as mobile and tactile as any ancient human.

The shuttle put me down in the ruins of a city known as Los Angeles, destroyed after ruptures in major fault-lines in the Earth's crust, led to virtual extinction of the human race. We knew that the species was only later saved by those living on the moons of Jupiter and Saturn whose descendants were to create our great cyborg dynasties.

I glided up the stairs of the ruined "Space Museum of Mankind" and inside found a circular auditorium from which a number of passages radiated. And at the end of one of these I found in a storeroom ancient records regarding manned space exploration from the very beginning of the "Space Age". A period so primitive that man had only recently managed to travel to Earth's own moon, less than two light seconds away!

What I learned there was astonishing given the purpose of my mission. For it confounded the idea that a probe from Earth could ever leave the galaxy because it showed early man never left the solar system!

The tapes showed that after the first moon landing fascination for manned flight faded as the public lost interest even when unmanned planetary fly-pasts showed undreamt of wonders. Funds for manned flight diminished whilst budgets boomed for satellite technology with its entertainment programmes. And using ideas and techniques acquired from space programmes humans explored parts of Earth, like the depths of the oceans, which seemed as fascinating as the large-scale cosmos, but for a fraction of the cost! Huge defense programmes soaked up vast resources ear-marked for manned flight and the universe was explored remotely using massive arrays of radio receivers helped by telescopes whirling in orbit around Earth, artificial probes and unmanned missions.

★ ★ ★

In spite of all this, the tape continued, some humans never abandoned the idea that man had a "divine right" to venture into space and this idea crystallised into a cult. Over the generations its funds increased until they were able to underwrite the huge cost of developing a "stellar-capable" craft whose first mission would be to voyage to the far reaches of the solar system before launching towards a nearby star system. The technology was still primitive, and the journey would take many hundreds of Earth years, and when they were at the limit of the sun's gravitational pull, the crew of six were advised by psychologists to "rest and reflect" for a month after which they would enter cryostasis and hibernate for the stellar voyage.

They all knew the Earth to which they hoped to return would differ greatly from the one they had left but were devoted to man's destiny. And with them they carried electronic "plaques" – messages to leave on other worlds bathed in the light of alien suns, proclaiming humanity's place in the life of the cosmos.

★ ★ ★

The next part of the tape consisted of brief quotes from crew members during the month of reflection. A few, arranged in chronological order, are set out below.

'I keep examining man's right to roam among the stars.'

'Asleep, I sense vivid dreams of which I have no recall.'

'I feel a sense that something important is coming.'

'On Earth nitrogen narcosis is called the "rapture of the deep", and here I think of as the "rapture of deep space".'

'I'm fearful of what lies beyond.'

'The "pale blue dot" of earth seems to be getting fainter.'

'Plagued by thoughts of empty space and infinity. Strong feeling of impending visit from *something*.'

'My mind is *emptying* – as if I'm being prepared for something.'

'It's here, I sense it, but there is no fear. Must be rational and say what I'm experiencing... a vaguely human shape but filmy. I doubt it has any form in our sense of a body. It's filling my mind with thoughts and warns us to go no farther. We're not equipped to cope with what's out there.'

'We all hear the message and the warning but we are determined to go on. Wish us well. Goodbye. Goodbye.'

★ ★ ★

When this information reached the group on Earth they regretted the loss of the crew but agreed that although man might yearn to adventure beyond Earth there was no evidence that included travel to the stars. Even so, they promoted solar-limited space programmes for men – those children of the rising and setting sun still had its family of planets and moons to explore and inhabit.

We cyborgs, their descendants, have travelled far and wide. But to say we have "conquered space" is a foolish notion – for just as early man could only explore the solar system so we, roaming with ease across the great star trails of our Galaxy can go no further than that. For there exists even for us, an unknown – possibly *unknowable* – censor, whether we like it or not. Absolute and undeniable.

As an early human I might have felt sad about that, but of course my neural circuits don't permit such flagrant feelings. But, as I said, my mental processes contain a *vestige* of humanity and the shred of emotion I feel, even as an advanced being, might be what humans would call "wistfulness". Not about the fate of the astronauts but about *ours* and the simple fact of knowing what these illogical and irrational beings did. For they elected to *go on* even knowing what they had been told and they have now been journeying for close on ten million Earth years.

Those who sent me to Earth had been charting their progress and calculated that they had just passed the point where they have left our Galaxy with the crew still in deep hibernation. And still carrying greetings from humanity to the Great Realms as we call them – the countless star – hoards of the universe.

And that's why I was sent to Earth to find out why they can go where we cannot. But I can't find a reason. Perhaps they were right all along about having a divine right to go "Beyond the utmost bound of human thought". And wistfulness? How can as unworthy a species as early man be able to travel among the Galaxies while we, such an advanced, rational and reasonable civilization grow old and die out in only one?

But while logic is limiting, *belief* is unhindered by reason. So all I will be able to take back to my seniors given that the unthinkable has happened and the craft and its crew go where we cannot is this: the craft is a symbol that man's destiny was to voyage for ever among all the stars in the universe and ours was not.

ICARUS UNBOUND

When Artificial Intelligence and advanced technology freed mankind from the shackles of thought, planning and actually *doing* anything, a desire arose in the breasts of some men to take to the skies. Not as machine handling aviators but as cyborgs – humans with biologically enhanced pectoral muscles, huge lungs and artificial wings.

Religious feeling opposed the idea maintaining that holy beings alone should be winged forgetting that Lucifer probably possessed as fine a clutch of flight feathers as any paid-up archangel. Other critics saw it as a fad but for some it was to be the first stage in *evolving* into something fundamentally different from flightless humans.

These early pioneers underwent extensive surgery to modify their bodies, greatly enhancing their metabolic rate to generate the power needed for flight. Diminished life expectancy was the penalty paid for the first to undergo such radical intervention, but as techniques improved these self-styled "avians" eventually lived as long as 'grounded' humans. And grafting wings and growing feathers just meant copying nature's perfect design for wing and tail feathers to propel, sustain and control flight.

In all some hundred thousand humans went along the "feathered route". But these superb aerial acrobats had no desire to become peepshows for the rest of humanity and chose to live together in remote natural locations existing on wild fruit and nuts. And it was clear that when sophisticated DNA manipulation became widely available an almost separate human species might evolve. And when it did, in time within the avian community an intense desire to *migrate* arose.

Humans had lived with birds too long to be amazed at the miracle of migration, and for earthbound man migrations were short, pasture-driven affairs. But many birds had routinely travelled thousands of miles a year and some were on the wing for most of their lives. Avians followed suit in adopting migration routes while some spent months on the move, never touching land.

At first "groundlings" were merely intrigued and then a deep feeling of "otherness" and resentment began to emerge. And after that it was only a question of time before some hunter aimed the bow whose arrow brought down the first avian. Others followed and soon no avian roamed the skies within the sight of man.

They disappeared – those who had soared and spun, effortlessly riding the great currents of air, disturbing no one and living in harmony. Critics said they had never created anything of lasting value and lived only for the moment, and it was true they never produced art and poetry but neither did they make guns, create armies or fight for the possession of property or land. Their critics were also mistaken for most such achievement is fleeting and those who saw them flying witnessed pure delight high among the clouds, surely as valid an achievement as anything created on earth.

The vast mass of humanity huddled below were ignorant of the loss of the priceless treasure above them in the skies, and few humans knew or cared what they had lost. Some said the few avians who survived were seen leaving from the west coast of America and flying towards the setting sun, but others said they'd watched them plunging in a graceful swirl into the heart of an active volcano in Hawaii. And a few deep-sea fishermen even reported seeing them flying off past the island of Spitzbergen going north.

But soon they were forgotten along with much else of beauty following the great disintegration of the Earth's economies when computers crashed, algorithms failed, democracy was exposed as the farce it had always been and there was no wisdom or willingness to repair or restore what was lost.

And then one day the avians were back bringing grace and beauty to adorn the skies. And even if Earth-bound humans had cared enough to look up, shading their eyes to catch a glimpse of their lost relations they would not have looked long. For they were simply too busy grubbing a living from the land and trying to survive in the Last Great Stone Age of Homo sapiens. A lengthy epoch from which humanity never completely emerged.

BIG PRICE - SMALL WONDER

y Gravi-car had gone in for a ten-year service and so I took a public Omni-Grav to work. Waiting for it at the station I picked up the kind of magazine I never usually read, called *A Galaxy of Gifts* with tiny star-systems flashing around on its cover. I thought it might help me choose a present for my niece who had an important anniversary coming up. She's a nano-neuro bacteriologist and pretty big in the world of small things and I wanted to find her something witty and whimsical.

After I'd boarded the O-G I opened the magazine at an article headed "Was Shakespeare an Alien?" and the well-dressed man sitting next to me glanced at what I was reading. I felt I had to explain why I'd bought it and he recommended I try a tiny gift shop in High Holborn near the old City of London boundary. Few such places still existed and there was usually a good reason why those that survived were still in business and so I said I'd pay them a visit.

'You'll need an introduction,' he said and gave me a card. 'Show them this,' he said. 'And they'll admit you, at once.'

I saw the card was blank and looked at him enquiringly.

'Don't worry they'll see things on that,' he said smiling, and I thanked him for his advice.

'Think nothing of it,' he said. 'It's really you I must thank for it's a long time since I met someone I could trust to go there.' And with that he shook my hand and disappeared into the crowd on the platform.

I found the shop tucked away in a small, gloomy alley and wondered if I'd come to the right place. The faded, old-fashioned front door was locked but when I pressed the brass button on the wall it generated a shrill ringing noise from deep inside. After a moment the door opened slowly with a bell-like "*ting*" and a tall, distinguished looking man wearing a frogged, velvet jacket peered at me over his half–moon spectacles.

'You have some form of… introduction, Sir?' he asked, and I proffered the card I'd been given. He scrutinized it carefully and then smiled warmly. 'You are most welcome,' he breathed. 'Such *impeccable* credentials.' He bowed slightly and ushered me through the shadowy passageway into a small, dark room lit by dim brass wall lamps on the linenfold panelling. There were no goods on display and only a sabre-legged chair placed before the counter on which rested a large blotting pad and an antique fountain pen.

'How may I assist you, Sir?' he asked, urging me to take a seat. 'Maltravers is my name, and I am entirely at your service. Was there anything in particular you are seeking?'

'I'm sorry to be so ill prepared,' Mr Maltravers,' I said. 'But I don't know what type of gifts you offer.'

'Scientific miniatures *definitely* not toys,' he shuddered. 'Oh, dear me, no. A universe of possibilities and all as *vibrant* as any real phenomena can be, anywhere.'

'Like a real star?'

'Nothing is beyond our capacity to give satisfaction and nature is always a *relative* matter. For example, black holes may be immense or microscopic.'

'Ut supra, ut infra,' I said. 'As above so below.'

'Rather a *clumsy* Latin phrase to my way of thinking, Sir,' he said, with a thin smile.

'Possibly a poor reflection of the Hermetic original,' I said, grinning broadly.

'And now, Sir...' he said briskly, but with a much warmer manner.

'I'm looking for something small but *weighty* to appeal to a young lady scientist. Nothing too elaborate, nothing too serious but nothing too...'

'Obvious,' he said, supplying the word I had in mind. 'Perhaps to mark a special occasion?'

'My niece. Twenty Thousand Sols, this Lunar.'

'A most delightful age,' he said, and then collecting himself, he continued. 'If you could me give an idea of the young person's tastes, I'm confident we'll find something suitable. We've just completed a stock-take and are offering many items at very reasonable prices.'

'Making room for the fresh and the new.'

'Precisely, Sir. We must all move with the times, or as the Bard has it: "time will waste us".'

'"Let not advantage slip,"' I said.

'Indeed, but tastes change over time,' he said, with a brief smile. 'And many of our newer customers seek items that only the *younger* galaxies can provide.'

'I was thinking about a smallish black hole for her,' I said laughing, for I still couldn't think he was serious. 'Not too short lived, but nothing too... violent.'

'An excellent idea, Sir. You have an eye for quality. But alas, your wise choice was pre-empted by a veritable *flurry* of demand for such items in our recent sale.'

'Clearly a "Black Friday".'

'Irrespective of the weekday or its colour our merchandise always attracts fierce competition at sale time,' he said. '"Fast movers" is the regrettable phrase used by Mr. Piers D'Arcy Pierce, our marketing consultant in one of his more sober moments.'

'Unobtainable then?'

'The few we have left are as rare as nebulaic gold dust, avidly sought by serious collectors and command correspondingly high prices.'

'How much might that mean?'

'May I suggest, Sir, with respect,' said Maltravers. 'That those serious about such items are usually indifferent to the financial side of the transaction.'

'I follow your drift,' I said. 'So what about an older, larger one?'

'Good value, of course – especially one pre-owned in good condition, but perhaps of greater appeal to an *older* person than your niece. And, of course they come without the guarantee of longevity that the more recent ones possess.'

'What else can you suggest?' I asked.

'Neutron stars are timeless in their appeal,' he said, permitting himself a diffident chuckle.

'Small but weighty like all good quality gifts.'

'Indeed, Sir,' he said. 'And often received with genuine appreciation as a thoughtful retirement gift in view of their relatively brief existence. But cherished they can last for many ages and many of them remain in the same family for years. Their collectors tend to be sociable beings, and a Neutron Star Convention is always one of the highlights of the galaxy season.'

'Perhaps something lighter?'

'How about a bright little nova – they have been known to gladden the heaviest heart,' he said. 'Or perhaps a modest, micro–supernova? Either represents a popular option for the groom to present to a potential bride of any gender or species.'

'Doesn't sound quite right for my niece.'

'May I ask if she is fond of travel?'

'Yes, she's always off somewhere. Why do you ask?'

'I can offer an attractively boxed virtual inter-galactic travel warrant with a very advanced in-built shape-shift capability and a hundred light years' travel range,' he said. 'Very appealing to the more *adventurous*.'

'Sounds a bit *active* to me,' I said. 'She told me in an unguarded moment that her secret wish was to give up science and become a librarian. But we're on the right track with a voucher for something.'

'Perhaps a "Planetoid in a Package", as we call it,' he said. 'Keep it at home in its "grow-bag" and watch it develop. It comes gift wrapped, fully guaranteed, licensed and limited to one per customer – a most rewarding and instructive offering.'

'Young people don't always have the patience or diligence to get the best out of a gift like that, I'm afraid.'

'Oh *how* I do agree, with you, Sir,' he tutted. 'Many goods are ruined because of lack of due diligence, with owners claiming ignorance about the need to employ a gravity-field replicator. I hasten to assure you that no one leaves us in any doubt on the matter.'

'People just don't listen.'

'Very true, Sir,' he said, with emotion. 'You can explain until the last star blinks out, that however good the seed, you can't expect a planetoid to thrive *wrenched* from its instinctual orbit without using an accredited gravitational compensatory device. And it needs feeding! No wonder the poor creatures die! Planetoids aren't just for Christmas, as the saying goes, whatever that was.'

'So you supply orbital devices?'

'Indeed we do and currently several are on special offer,' he said. 'Very popular with our Japanese customers. But then they care for all things miniature, especially planetsai.'

'The idea of a small heavenly body appeals to me,' I said. 'But wouldn't a young person find one a bit *dull*?'

'Who are we to fathom the inclinations of those with different tastes, Sir,' he said, with a sparkle in his eye. 'But we stock planetoids in all sizes with various features and I understand young people currently favour ones with geysers that shoot out unexpectedly from their surface and have themed gatherings where they guess where the next geyser will erupt from the sphere's surface. Those who get it badly wrong have to take their face masks off. A little *risqué* to my taste but doubtless very exciting!'

'Anything else in your economy range?'

'Some rather *faded* time-warp trips to the sulphur mines of Mercury,' he said. 'Which I would hesitate to recommend to you. A virtual "sunrise surprise" pack from a planet with nineteen suns all appearing at the same time – I can give you a *very* good price on that. Or you might prefer a similar trip around the event horizon of a black hole. There's also a novelty box of cosmic frequencies which can transport you virtually to the origin of any selected wavelength.'

'I think I'll go for a small planetoid and an orbit rectifier.'

'Very good choice, Sir,' he said, and disappeared to find one. But when he returned it was with a look of profound regret.

'Sadly the last one went yesterday,' he said. 'However I think I have here a worthy substitute.' He held out a cardboard box labelled "Planet Seeds", with "Ages: Five Thousand to Adult" written above a picture of a humanoid boy grinning at a planet in his hand while his father looked on, positively drooling with pride.

'I'm assured that seeding a planet without a "grow-bag" is the very latest craze among the more mature young,' he said. 'With the right nutrient – as supplied – you can grow your own mini-planet anywhere from a single seed, and if that appeals you can add others without limit. I understand some of our established customers now own quite complex star systems.'

'But you can't just go around creating matter just like that can you?'

'The authorities are acutely aware of the dangers,' he said. 'And you need a license to use the seeds. Underage possession is forbidden as is ownership of the "Good God Creator Companion Manual". And there are strict controls governing the number and size of planets and moons you can grow. Happily "planet-masters" as they call themselves are usually content to confine their collections to a small handful of planets with their moons.'

'May I order one with a solar system limit?'

'By all means, Sir,' he beamed. 'Will you take them in the packet or gift wrapped? If you choose the former, please exercise extreme caution carrying them as any hint of planet droppings on the pavement carries a very stiff penalty!'

'I'll bear that in mind,' I said, trying to keep a straight face. 'If I got home and found a seed missing, what could I say to my niece? It would make a world of difference to my gift!'

'A "lost world", indeed, Sir,' he said, with a twinkle in his eye. 'And to think of you lost for words as well! A high price indeed for us all to have to pay!'

KEEPING IT
IN THE FAMILY

Right here, on the rim of the crater outside the dome, is the very spot on Mars where I sat of an evening after terraforming had made the air breathable. The crater was called, "Tycho Impact" after the one on the moon and the surface was pinky-red, like a desert on Earth but without near Venusian temperatures!

I remember so clearly *being* here at first but not *getting* here. None of that tedious business of packing, farewells or the flight itself.

'Dad, you need rest and quiet,' my eldest boy, Fred, had said on the voice-com, soon after the embarrassing episode at my tri-centennial gathering on Earth. He didn't sound too happy having been forced by the family to confront me.

'So where do you suggest I get that?' I'd replied.

'The Moon?' he said, hopefully.

'That's the family talking through you, Son, isn't it?' I said. 'They'd like nothing better than to dump me down some disused nickel quarry retirement complex for geriatrics.'

After my reply his connection seemed to go on the blink while two thousand linked relatives girded up their loins.

Then the old coven of witch-wives got tough with him and he stumbled on.

'Titan, one of Saturn's moon's popular for seniors,' he said. 'It's got hydrocarbon lakes and... wait for it: methane rain and snow.' Off stage I heard lots of "ohs" and "ahhs", and the odd "bless him".

I told them where he could put their methane snow and felt the family tightening its collective lips.

'Or Enceladus's *really* good,' he labored on, 'Just beautiful – the "Fairest of Saturn's Children".'

'I wouldn't survive the trip,' I said. 'You forget I've only got two hearts and one of them's dodgy.' Few humans were as challenged as me because most people had several duplicate organs implanted as microdots in their buttocks.

Some bright spark then thought of Mars.

'*Mars!*' I remember, shouting it out. 'I may be old, but I'm not ready for the greatest collection of boring old farts from here to Pluto.'

'Now Pluto's a thought,' said a voice I recognised as coming from a cretinous woman I'd once married in a Canadian hellhole called New Nebraska.

'I'll pretend I didn't hear, that.'

'Have you any idea of how much it is to send even a *small* parcel there,' said a posh voice from Maryland, Labrador. 'Just getting him there would cost a fortune, and think of the insurance.'

'Well here's one parcel who won't be freezing its wrappings off,' I said, before the family viragos started chiming in.

'So why have they got a waiting list a parsec long?' chimed in someone from the Michigan Peninsular Riviera.

'Why not just send me to a bungalow in the Oort Cloud and be done with it,' I said, regretting it, as I spoke.

'Let's be reasonable,' said a gentle voice, belonging to one of my early spouses, Rose Gamma, a pretty Innuit girl, forced from her home by the bush fires raging over the southern part of Hudson's Bay. Nice girl and much sought after for her fishing skills, I recalled. And much else too.

'*I'm* willing to compromise, but don't forget I'm not the superman I was when we were "Young Brave and Melting Squaw".'

'This isn't getting us anywhere,' chimed in a wife whose number I forgot, but whose rasping tones had stayed with me for what seemed like an eternity. 'Let's take him out of the hearing loop and vote on where he's going. Don't forget it'll be at our expense for goodness knows how long.'

The line then went blank and the next thing a squad of white coats from Geriatrics Anonymous broke into my house on Earth as I was entertaining a few lady friends and sedated me. And when I woke up here I was on terra-formed Mars.

★ ★ ★

'Hallo Dad,' said a voice on the intercom. 'Eddie here – your eldest now that Fred's passed on.'

'What do you want?' I said, smelling a rat. 'I'm not bothering any of you.'

'It seems very quiet there,' he said, scanning my crater.

'It is,' I said. 'Only us here, and that's how we like it.'

'There's a reason it's only you there.'

'Is there?' I said, puzzled. 'I assumed it was bought by the family and chosen to keep me quietly out of the way.'

'Not *quite* true – for a start the dome's rented – and very reasonably for double occupation.'

Where's this going? I thought.

'In spite of the impact clause,' he said, hesitantly and stopped.

'Impact clause! What impact clause?'

'Nothing to worry about,' he said. 'Just a very low probability that you'd get a visitor in your lifetime. Anyway, I think they only called it a high-risk impact zone to hike up the rent because of the high insurance premiums they said they had to pay.'

'What sort of "visitor"?'

'Oh, maybe once in a blue moon a small meteor might turn up. I mean a tiny *meteorite,* a minute speck of space debris.'

'*Turn up!*' I shouted. 'You mean hit the crater at twenty-thousand miles an hour. Well, thanks for telling me, *Son.* Am I to understand the family condemned me to live out my remaining centuries in some high-risk, hellhole?'

'I'm sure it wasn't like that.'

'Have you any idea of the damage a mote of dust can do to a space-suit?' I shouted.

'Think positively,' he pleaded, but I moved in for the kill.

'It's hardly any time since I came here, and now you want to shuffle me off to some penal planet like Neptune.'

'Dad, when you first came to your crater,' said Eddie, 'Remember the height of the rim mountains?'

'Yes, I do,' I almost choked, thinking about it.

'And do you remember when we asked how long you'd be there you said. 'Until the highlands are just a dusty plain?'

'And what can you see now?'

'A rim of mountains.'

'But it *looks* more worn down to me on my scanner,' he said. 'You've had a good run here, but Mars prices are taking off and they won't renew the lease on the same terms. Come back to us, be part of your family.'

'No fear, I like it here, I love the solitude.'

'But we may not be able to keep you here much longer,' he said. 'The family's had a rough time recently and we've already defaulted once on the payments to keep you there.'

'How bad is it?'

'They're threatening to turn off the water and re-possess the dome.'

'They can't do that. Can they?'

'Yes, they can,' he said. 'How do you fancy a condo on Titan? We hear they're very nice, and we could run to a little double-domed apartment, there. Not new but done up really nicely.'

'You think I want to go to *Titan* and mix with a load of old dossers from the scrapings of the solar system?'

'Eddie – if you won't tell him, I will,' said a fresh voice, belonging to the very worst of my many awful wives. I knew that tone of old and listened with a feeling of dread.

'Listen, you old codger,' she said. 'If it's not going to be Titan with Rose, it's the Moon with me, or Kansas on Earth with dear Eric and Edith. *If* they'll have you. Take it or leave it.'

'You did say a *double*-domed apartment, on Titan, didn't you, my dear boy?'

'Guaranteed,' he said. 'Plenty of room for you and good for entertaining.'

'Sigh me up, Son,' I said with a heavy heart.

And that brings me full circle to my sitting here for the last evening looking out over our crater. It's Titan for me tomorrow, and then what? Who knows? I might even think of settling down with a nice lady if I meet one. I usually do.

THE MEDIUM IS THE MESSAGE

The early part of the twenty-first century on Earth was an uncomfortable time for many people in the west starting with an american president with a slender grasp on reality enrapturing tens of millions of voters in his pursuit of populist support. A brief respite followed owing to a world-wide viral pandemic before a Russian president invaded a sovereign country and justified his action as historical obligation. And common sense took another holiday when woke warriors, uncomfortable with selected aspects of the past, tinkered around with its legacy rather than moving on to better things.

England, for once taking the initiative then helped create a brief period later referred to as the "New Enlightenment". "Facts" became the new fashion, its adherents replacing opinion peddlers, self-disclosure egoists and the incontinent blurtings of self-styled "influencers". And although the unearthing of verifiable facts through rigorous inquiry remained as elusive as ever, "science" and its more persuasive practitioners enjoyed celebrity status. Politicians, ever quick to feel the pulse of the electorate began employing empty phrases like "objective verifying" to give apparent credence to the truth, and newspaper editors instructed journalists to stick to reliable reporting of actual newsworthy events.

Academics could call the era what they liked but this new rational climate created opportunities for thoughtful people like Pete and me.

'This is our big moment after wasting our talents for so long on a thankless public.' I said to him. 'Now we can *diversify* the business without sacrificing our hard-won reputation for quality service.'

'Right-on, Mart!' said Pete, my buddy and partner, giving me a high five.

At the time we were engaged in a business called "Domestic Streamlining Unlimited", a niche version of what was vulgarly referred to as "house clearances". This enabled us to channel some of the items that came our way into a small boutique offering objects d'art in an Antique Arcade adjacent to the Portobello Road Market in London's Notting Hill.

Although we were "Mart and Pete" to our friends we traded as "Michel and Pierre" and rubbed along with our Fine Art business neighbours, privately educated and immaculately tailored lay-abouts who tolerated our rougher trade presence in their midst. Not only by supplying them with expensive looking tat from our clearances but because we shared a common interest in making a profit from the greed and opportunism of the average punter always negotiating worthless "bargains".

Polly, a pretty, practical woman and her glamorous wife Fiona, who we fondly referred to as "mystic and lipstick", were an exception to this dismal bunch, They ran a "Cosmic Contact and Spiritual Alignment Agency", basically a clearing house for those wishing to embrace spiritualism in one of its many forms. We all got on famously and often shared a bottle or two of wine with them when the arcade had closed for the day and the other stallholders had gone home.

'Ladies,' I said, one evening. 'Michel speaking so listen up.'

'We're all ears, *Marty* darling,' said Polly, grinning in that irritating way people did when I was trying to be serious.

'In the light of the current societal renaissance,' I said casting her one of my looks, 'I would like to introduce the subject of "evidence based" investigation of the spirit world.'

'Bit of a contradiction in terms, I'd have thought,' said Fiona. 'How would it work?'

'Mart and me get to clear out all sorts of places,' said Pete. 'And sometimes it's broken-down junk that doesn't work but looks impressive.'

'Like old juke boxes, record players and even early fridges.' I said. 'Not to mention even older stuff like wartime radar equipment.'

'Take your spiritual customers who want to contact their dear departed,' said Pete, pouring into his beaker half a bottle of Chateauneuf. 'If we wired up a few bits of equipment we thought it might look to the punters like we was using science to contact spirits in the next world.'

'An electronic communication channel as a kind of spiritual chat line,' I said.

'And make it a bit *fuzzy* so they can't tell it's not old Auntie Mabel on the other end of the blower, like,' said Pete.

As you can tell from these few snatches of dialogue Pete's contribution to our business lay more in the heavy lifting department rather than Brain Central, which was more my side of things.

'It's a perfect example of the "medium being the message",' I said. '"All's well here and hoping you are, too", from the other side of the grave usually keeps customers happy.'

'And helpful advice to punters from wise souls,' said Pete, thinking of his own situation. 'Like telling you to mind your back when you lift something. Everyone over thirty will agree with that and think it applies only to them.'

'Words of help and hope,' I said. 'Spreading a bit of happiness in this dismal age.'

'A public service, like,' added Pete.

'It's awful and you both know it,' cried Polly. 'Preying on the simple minded like that is cynical and immoral. You should be ashamed of yourselves.'

'So you won't help us get clients then?' said Pete, hopefully.

'Pol didn't say that,' said her wife, hurriedly.

★ ★ ★

After a few more drinks we agreed to hire some bigger premises and use most of the space to house a load of scientific looking equipment we'd stockpiled from the clearance business. And I had another supplier in mind, a cousin of mine, we called "Runabout Rigby", who owned a junkshop, specialising in electrical goods and was good at making things work, at least as far as the door to his shop. And if he could make some of our old things light up and the parts move about a bit we thought he would be ideal for what we called "Operation Psychic Insights".

Pol and Fi were still not too happy about the ethics of our operation and we needed to clear the air.

'We'll only relay happy or helpful messages,' I said, reassuringly.

'Honest,' said Pete

'You'd better,' said Fi. 'If you want any help from us. Go on Pol, tell the rascals what to do.'

'You'll need to operate like a studio,' said Polly. 'With telephone contact at first, moving to "zoom mode" as quickly as possible after that.'

So we got Rigby to design a way of automatically transferring a simple phone contact to this format with me sitting at a desk behind which was Pete, wearing the white coat we called boffin wear, delicately adjusting dials and knobs surrounded by the flashing lights of his "scientific" instruments.

'Ask your clients to give brief details of who they want to contact and what they want to know,' said Polly. 'Then tell them you'll prepare a "Psycho algorithm" and after some further input from you they'll be connected to them in some mysterious way, devised by Rigby, to a pre-recorded blurred message from their dear departed.'

It worked well in practice but we found it was the *medium* – the "scientific" *contact* that really impressed the punters rather than the *message* which was hard to decipher and pretty anodyne, anyway. And to be fair I'd researched everything from ectoplasm to exorcism and could handle most of their queries about the occult. I also tried to understand what Rigby had done but to no avail. I doubt if he understood half of what he was doing, anyway.

After seeing we were making folk happy, Pol and Fi, were helpful in finding us suitable clients, which we did on a strictly business basis. They got a cut for introductions, but we agreed they'd never have to compromise themselves or say anything more than we were *hoping* to apply scientific methods to psychic phenomena.

★ ★ ★

After a shaky start, things went quite well as the clients referred to us were undemanding and pleased with our limited service. But after a while we started getting some strange transmissions from "future" spirits. *Odd that,* we thought. We'd set up a service for living people wanting contact with the spirits of those who had passed on, but getting people from the future wanting access to us in their *past* was really weird.

Apparently, people from some futures looked back to our brief golden period of rationality with longing as future society didn't seem to be any better at preventing people from being lonely and unhappy than ours. *All well and good* we thought but how to cope with this rising flood of spiritual traffic? We knew we were already giving a useful service to our existing clientele and value given justified the financial returns we got. However such "returns from the future" needed careful handling for spirits coming from a variety of times and different places were often capricious and needed careful handling as the following case in "futures" illustrates.

The woman came through one Tuesday afternoon when I was putting up my feet for a well-earned rest and reading an improving piece of pulp-fiction. I should mention that Rigby had fitted up an amplification system, so it was like communicating with Alexa. We'd also adopted an electronic recognition address.

'Hello, Gremlin 3,' she said using my call sign. Pretty cool and classy, we thought.

'Come in Ethereal 23,' I said. 'Please identify yourself, your era, your current Earthly address or planetary location.'

'I'm Sorgette, a female humanoid from Earth in the 3rd Ice age,' she said.

'Can you be more specific?' I asked. 'Relate it to my era? Over.'

'You're in Interglacial period 2,' she said. 'What we call the "warm, dark ages".'

'Copy that,' I said. We didn't know what that meant, but it always sounded good. 'How can I help you?'

'By telling me how come you're using a way of communicating that we've only just discovered,' she said.

'Excuse me asking,' I said. 'But let me just get this straight. As far as I know an Interglacial Period is about 10,000 years long so you must be at least 25,000 years in my future.'

'That sounds about right,' said Sorgette. 'So what?'

'There's another thing I need to ask you,' I said.

'Which is?'

'Are you living or dead?'

'I'd hardly be speaking to you if I was dead now would I?' she said. 'Is there someone else I can talk to there?'

'Let me explain,' I said, and I told her who we were, what we did and who we had to deal with from the future. I was keen to know what she wanted but didn't want to sound too eager and was beginning to wish Pete didn't always go to the Gay Gigolo Pool Parlour in the early afternoons.

'It sounds as if one of your pseudo-scientific gizmos is generating a breakthrough in temporal communication,' she said.

'Don't forget you're talking to someone who's been dead for millennia,' I said. 'So if you don't mind I'll just sign off.' I couldn't see any mileage in talking to some entity so far in the future who didn't seem to qualify for any of our services.

'Wait!' she said. 'This is an enormous breakthrough, and you're going to throw it away.'

'Look Madam, Sorgette or E23. I've no idea which bit of our equipment has done this because they're all just junk to impress our customers.'

'But *something* works!'

'OK *it* works, but I'm not working now, am I?' I said. 'And time's money.' I can be very financially focused sometimes.

'Can I do something to ensure you'll keep the connection open?'

'Money always helps.'

'How much would you need?'

'What do you use in your Ice Age for pound notes?' I said. 'Icicles? Snowballs?'

'If you send me an image of your equipment,' she said. 'Maybe we can work out how to send you some money.'

'How do I get the photo to you?'

'I expect you're using some Stone-Age device like a small computer, aren't you?'

'Yes. Reconditioned, but state of the art three years ago,' I said, proudly. 'I suppose that's thirty thousand years ago to you.'

'Are you sure there isn't anyone else there I could speak to.'

My finger hovered over the "off" button but I retained the calm and poise for which I'm pretty famous.

'Use it to send over the image in the usual way and leave us to do the clever stuff,' she said. And so I sent over a camera shot of our equipment.

'Describe all these devices to me,' she said. 'But first tell me how they are connected.'

I showed her the multi-socket point that transmitted power to the machines and then explained what I thought was their original purpose. One looked like a mirror used by actors when they're making up with a ring of bulbs around the sides. Another was a green, dim screen looking like a radar scanner from the last war before ten that showed dots moving together for some reason. In another corner was something that looked like an old jukebox, and next to it was a one armed bandit where the winnings fell down with a clatter of coins into a metal tray. I didn't tell her that the mechanism was a bit intermittent and sometimes got stuck with three oranges in a row. There was even an old cash dispenser machine salvaged after a ram raid robbery.

'Our clients are impressed by these,' I said. 'They add authenticity to our mission, the veracity of which some are incapable of appreciating without such support.'

'It's all rubbish and you know it. Where did you get it?'

'I'm not sure I like your tone. What kind of people are you?'

'The kind who'll pay you anything you ask if you keep the contact open,' she said. 'I'm now linked up to others in the cavern who are searching your data base and seeing your pictures. They say I can materialise some banknotes if you send us an image of what you want. When we've worked out how to do it maybe we can send them using the cash dispenser. But you'll have promise to keep the link open.'

'That sounds good,' I said, frantically fishing around for a fifty-pound note that had to last me until the next injection of income from some unknown source.

'How many of those things do you want?' she said, scanning my image.

'Five hundred for a start. Only new ones, please, and while I think about it you can credit my bank account as well. I'll type in the number.'

'How much do you want put into your account?'

'Ten million pounds,' I said sending her the number.

'Before we send you the money, tell us where the equipment comes from.'

'From this supplier,' I said giving them the address. It didn't seem necessary to explain that it was a junkshop owned by my cousin Rigby. Or that he'd left the country.

'E-mail?' she said, and I gave it. 'That all checks out,' she said. 'You'll find we've put a hundred pounds into your account.'

'A *hundred* pounds!' I said. 'What about the rest?'

'We may be iced up, but we're not stupid, you nasty, greedy little man.'

'That does it! I'm breaking off all contact with you, and you've only yourselves to blame!'

'That's not going to happen,' she said. 'We've been working on this connection as we spoke and now you're hard-wired to us. And I hope for his sake your cousin is going to be more helpful than you.'

'How did you find out about him?'

'We can also read your mind,' she said. 'It's not much but it'll have to do for now. It won't be difficult to find something better, and we'll pay a lot more than a hundred pounds for that, you can be sure. Copy that.'

I was speechless! A dead liberty, I call it. How can you earn an honest penny dealing with people like that? And so much for the New Enlightenment, with its fancy ideas about science! It makes you want to go back to those golden days of inspired leadership when everything was perfect. Lots of bold new ideas and honest opinions from interesting folk and not a damned fact in sight!

★ ★ ★

'Don't expect any sympathy from us,' said Polly when I told her what had happened. 'She sounds like a very focused level-headed businesswoman. You'd better let one of us speak to her and I'll see what can be salvaged from this whole sorry mess.'

That was nostalgia in spades for me – it was just like speaking to my ex wives all at once.

'If you think it'll do any good just try it and see,' I said, climbing out of my chair. 'And here's the equipment you can use.'

Then I stumbled out of the studio and had a heavy session in the Travellers Rest.

When I came in next day, I noticed that our professional atmosphere of careless informality had changed dramatically. There were flowers on the tidy desk, someone had put up window blinds and there was a photo on *my* desk of Pol and Fi on their honeymoon.

Aghast I ventured into the science room and looked around to see what mayhem had taken place there. Then I gathered that Pol had come back to the studio for I heard her voice.

'Now Sorgette,' she was saying. 'Make sure the mixture's nice and *fluid* before you put it outside the cave. The secret is to let it solidify *slowly* and then your ice will be just perfect.'

'Tell her that adding a few berries on top always adds that little touch,' said Fiona.

'What's going on?' I said, unable to believe my ears.

'Ask Pete,' Polly said. 'He gets in earlier than you.'

'Well?' I said 'Dawn riser, what have you got to say?'

'They seem to have saved your bacon,' he said, smiling at Polly and Fiona.

'So you're in the food line as well?' I said. 'Turncoat.'

'No, way, Mart,' said Pete. 'Pol spoke to this Sorgette woman, and they sort of clicked. And after a while they were talking recipes for some crummy cavern dinner party, she's throwing.'

'*Recipes!*' I heard someone shouting and then realised it was me. 'We're in the world of temporal time-shift and teleport communication,' I screamed. '*Man's* stuff. Muscle and mind, not knitting patterns and flower arranging.'

'We might have got it slightly wrong about that, Mart,' said Pete. 'Seems all the cock-ups in history are literally man-made. And the future's…'

'What? The future's what?'

'Feminine,' he said shakily, with a weak smile.

'Like hell, it is!'

But later when they let me get back into the studio I'll tell you one thing – the baked Alaska that old Sorgette cooked in her cave and sent a sample to us through the cash dispenser machine, although a bit *attenuated* was to die for!

'Whoever said the way to a man's heart was through his stomach was dead right,' said Pete taking a last mouthful.

'Now *there's* an opportunity staring us in the face,' I said. 'With Sorgette's cave connections I can see a great future for us Pete my lad. We'll market her food to busy housewives throughout the land.'

'Eh,' he said.

'I can picture it now,' I said, seeing dazzling displays and deathless prose: "Frozen Treats From Ice Age Kitchen – Cavern Cool and Table Ready".